Praise for *The Lies We Tell*

"Holland...demonstrates her honest sensitivity to the extremes of youthful vanity and the limits of parental responsibility... A warm novel...." – Kirkus Reviews

"To subtle but startling effect, Holland roots her delicate coming-of-age story squarely in the middle of a perfectly rendered 1970's. Against a backdrop of large-scale deceit, thirteen-year-old Martie, struggling with grief, learns what a nation learned: truth can break your heart even as it sets you free." –Marisa de los Santos, author of *Love Walked In* and *Belong to Me*

"Jamie Holland is a strong, fresh, powerful new voice in fiction. From the very first page *The Lies We Tell* instantly pulls you in to 1974 and the vivid, mesmerizing, heart-felt world of thirteen-year-old Martie Wheeler. This is one character, one book, you won't forget." –Jessica Anya Blau, author of *The Summer of Naked Swim Parties* and *The Wonder Bread Summer*

"Anyone who stumbled through middle school is bound to relate to the protagonist in Jamie Holland's haunting and evocative *The Lies We Tell*. An adult writing the voice of a child is a daunting task but with her pared-down prose and airtight storytelling, Holland makes it look effortless. Told with the backdrop of the Watergate crimes and the upheaval of the 1970s, *The Lies We Tell* is not just a good coming-of-age story, it is a great novel, period." –Julia Slavin, author of *Carnivore Diet* and *The Woman who Cut off her Leg at the Maidstone Club and Other Stories*

"A hidden gem of a book. Through shy, observant Martie we rediscover what it's like to be thirteen again: the pain when the people we love change, the confusion of shifting allegiances, the intense desire to be somebody, *anybody.* It's the kind of crossover coming-of-age story we need more of, written from the perspective of a young narrator who's just beginning to find her power and her voice. Holland writes like the wise and quirky offspring of Judy Blume and Wes Anderson." —Rebecca Flowers, author of *Nice to Come Home to*

"In her wonderful debut, *The Lies We Tell,* Jamie Holland has created a memorable and endearing protagonist. Martie's humorous observations and unflinching quest for truth draw us in and make us hold our breath as she confronts the grief, and secrets, that engulf her heart-broken family." — Karen Day, author of *Tall Tales* and *A Million Miles from Boston*

The Lies We Tell

A NOVEL

Jamie Holland

ISBN: 0692300449
ISBN 13: 9780692300442
Library of Congress Control Number: 2015907328
Jamie Holland, Washington, D.C.

Acknowledgments

THE SEED FOR this book was sown in a 1992 Jenny McKean Moore workshop in Washington, D.C., taught by the wonderful writer, Carole Maso.

I'm grateful to my sixth grade English teacher, Miss Kopp, for instilling a love of reading and writing as well as a passion for diagramming sentences. A very big thanks to my first creative writing teacher, C.W. Smith, who encouraged me to keep writing, and to Richard Peabody, who published my first short story in *Gargoyle*.

Boundless gratitude to those who supported me for years through numerous revisions, serious bouts of self-doubt and unfailing willingness to read "just one more draft." Especially Michelle Brafman, Rebecca Flowers and Paulette Roberts.

I thank my mother for driving us to the library on a regular basis and my father for reciting poetry whenever the spirit moved him. Special thanks to Carey for the annual supply of steno books and to Kris for letting me borrow her clothes as well as her Harlequin romances. Both sisters inspired the book's point of view.

My wise-beyond-their-years teenage readers—Sasha, Beya, Ravenna, Isadora and Althea—offered mature insight and sincere enthusiasm when I needed it most.

Lastly, and most importantly, to Edward, who, for years, has quietly and generously given me the time and space to write, and done so with an abundance of faith, patience and love.

For Sasha and Beya

Chapter 1

FOUR MONTHS AFTER my father died, I told my mom that I wanted to see a psychiatrist.

"A psychiatrist?" she said from the driver's seat of our station wagon. "How did you get that idea? Do you know someone who sees a psychiatrist?"

The radio was low, but I could hear the guy saying something about Watergate.

"No." I picked at a ragged cuticle. A curl of skin fell to my bare thigh and I flicked it off. I stuck my arm out the window and spread my fingers wide, then cupped my hand to catch the warm Maryland air. Already it felt like summer even though it was only the end of April.

Mom stopped at a red light and turned my way. "You can't talk to me?"

"No, it's not that," I lied, thinking, *I've tried, but you never want to.* "It's just…" I turned to the side mirror. Tiny beads of sweat clustered around my hairline.

The reporter's voice got louder as he said, "And now President Nixon is even more deeply engaged in fighting the most difficult political battle of his life."

"Is it about your father?" Mom asked.

Of course it was about him. The whole thing didn't make sense. A healthy person didn't just drop dead from a heart attack. But Blaire and Mom didn't want to talk about it. They were like, *He died, okay? Let it go.* Well, I couldn't.

Behind us, a car honked. Mom flipped on her blinker and made a hasty right turn, which led us into a fancy neighborhood where, in fifth grade my best friend, Robin, and I trick or treated and returned home with twelve Hershey bars each. Now cherry blossoms filled the street, their branches pink and fluffy as cotton candy.

"Speaking of your father," Mom said, smoothing her hand over her thick, brown hair that frizzed and curled with the humidity the same way mine did. "I might need to get a new job."

I readjusted my glasses. "What kind of job?" She'd been a real estate agent forever, but in the past few years she'd mentioned needing to make more money.

"Oh, I don't know," she sighed, slowing down at a red light. "We'll just have to see."

I placed my hand against my chest and counted the beats. "Do we not have enough money?"

The concealer under Mom's eyes that was meant to hide the evidence of sleepless nights shone in the afternoon sun.

She patted my bare leg. "We'll be all right, Martie. Don't worry."

But I did, and I would.

Across the street was a white house with black shutters, a wraparound porch and wicker furniture the color of pistachio ice cream. A real estate sign was stuck in the front yard. I waited for Mom to comment on how much it might be worth or what it might sell for, but she just stared at the house, a glazed look settling deep in her eyes.

"Mom?"

She turned to me. Her new, frosty lipstick lent her a pale, flat look.

"It's green," I said.

She blinked. "Oh." She stepped on the accelerator and we lurched forward. She drove fast, almost missed our turn, then accidentally swerved, nearly sideswiping a blue station wagon with wood paneling on the side.

"Are you okay?" I asked.

Stupid question. Of course she wasn't okay. None of us were. Just last week she'd slammed on her brakes, skidding into the car ahead of us. What if Mom crashed into a tree and died? No. Nothing worse would happen to us. I said it over and over, *That was enough, that was enough, nothing worse will happen*, like a nursery rhyme, until Mom pulled in front of our small Tudor house and we carried the groceries inside and turned on the local news.

Chapter 2

"THE SUDDEN DISAPPEARANCE of two young girls from the Montgomery Mall has left the community shaken," the dark haired reporter with the thick sideburns said. "It's now been a grueling forty-eight hours for the anxious parents."

Mom hurried to the black and white T.V. that sat atop our refrigerator. "You don't want to see this. It's an awful story."

"No!" I rushed in front of her. "I wanna see it."

"It's terrible. You shouldn't watch it."

"Yes, I should." I turned up the volume.

The guy went on to report that the Hanley sisters, ten and twelve, had last been seen two days ago at the mall, eating French fries and talking to a mustached man who was doing coin tricks. Robin and I had been to that mall a million times, so I could picture the girls sitting at one of those wobbly tables outside of Surrey's Burgers and Fries. But I didn't get how someone could've taken them from such a public place. Or maybe the guy followed them as they walked home and then pushed them into his car.

A picture appeared on the television screen—two blondes with ponytails, laughing and squinting in the sun.

Before the broadcast ended, the dad came on. He wore a dark suit and a wide tie like my dad used to wear every single day.

He looked right into the camera and said he'd do anything to get their little girls back—"absolutely anything"—and then the camera cut to the news guy with the sideburns. Patty Hearst had been kidnapped a few months ago, but that was different—she was nineteen. And that serial killer out in California had been murdering young women for the past two years, but the Hanley girls were young. Practically my age.

Our front door budged, then came a wave of heat, followed by the soft thud of Blaire's tennis shoes. She was sixteen, had perfect skin, long legs and a cute boyfriend named Danny who was a basketball star. They were the perfect couple; even my seventh grade classmates idolized them.

"What?" she said when she saw us in the kitchen. She glanced up at the T.V., tossed her tennis racquet on a chair and said, "Oh yeah. The Hanleys. Someone at school used to babysit for them."

"It's terrible," Mom said, shaking her head.

"How does everyone know about this except me?"

Blaire pointed to the screen. "Because it's right there on the news. Duh."

I flipped on the sink faucet and poured a stream of Ivory dish soap into my palms. "What if they die?" My mind screeched from one horrible scenario to the next—the girls tied to trees, the girls being strangled to death.

Normally I'd call Robin so we could freak out about it together, but after school she and her mom had gone downtown to get passports. Her whole family was going to Singapore for the entire summer because her dad was in charge of some project over there. He worked for the State Department, but still I didn't get why the parents had to drag the kids there, too.

The phone rang, blaring through our tiny kitchen, revving up my heart and setting my whole body on high alert. Lately everything startled me—the click of the dishwasher starting a new cycle, the bell at school, the slam of a locker door.

It was Dad's sister, Aunt Julie. She lived in Wisconsin.

The two of them had been having marathon phone conversations for months. From Mom's end, I'd hear scattered words, like "I know" and "He was. It's true." Then sniffing, usually. Julie had stayed with us after Dad died, helping with funeral arrangements and all that. More than once, I'd caught her eying Blaire in a worried way like Blaire was the only one affected by what had happened.

Mom pulled the tan twirly phone cord all the way into the dining room until it was taut. I strained to hear, but she talked in a very low voice.

"No, not yet," she said.

Ten minutes into the conversation, the crying started. Over the years, I'd grown accustomed to the occasional tear dribbling down her cheek, but now her crying was like a choking deep inside, coming from a place I never knew existed.

Last week I overheard her say, "Sometimes I feel like I'm being crushed from all sides."

I ran to the bathroom, grabbed an extra roll of toilet paper from under the sink and handed it to her just in time to hear her whisper, "I know. I need to tell them."

—⊷⊶—

In bed all I thought was, Tell us *what?* Did she know something about the Hanley girls? I couldn't get it out of my mind that two innocent girls could walk to the mall one spring afternoon and not return home. It was exactly what had happened to Dad—he went to work and he didn't come home. All that was left was his half-filled coffee cup in the sink and his clothes and suits in the upstairs closet.

The air in our room was suffocating. Tonight would be another night of tossing and turning, my warm body desperate to locate cool spots on my sheets. The pathetic fan between our beds blew a few wisps of my hair. We had one air conditioning unit in the house and it was in Mom and Dad's room. Well, Mom's room.

"Where do you think that guy took them?" I asked Blaire, who laid on her side, reading an autobiography of Arthur Ashe.

"I dunno." She turned the page. Her hair was long and brown, but soon the summer sun would turn a strip in the front totally blonde. She'd pull that piece back with a barrette so that there'd be this perfect blonde streak going across the brown. It killed me how good she looked without trying. My hair, just for the record, had once been described by my mother as the color of dishwater. And my glasses, according to Blaire, made me look like a confused owl.

Photos of Danny covered her wall—"Dannyland," I called it—Danny in a pool, Danny playing basketball, Blaire on Danny's lap. He had blonde hair that swooped over his forehead, a deep dimple in his left cheek and very white teeth. Sometimes I stood in front of the pictures with my lips puckered, imagining we were kissing. Earlier in the year, Matt Fleming and I shared a peck on the mouth, but that was the extent of my kissing experience.

"What do you think he said to them?" I asked, imagining all the lines Mom had warned us about: *Can you help me find my puppy? Want some candy? Come see the surprise in my car!*

I sat up. "I mean, to get both girls in the car, he must've—"

"*Sh.* I'm *read*ing."

I turned away from her and my eyes landed on the brown smear against the wall where last week Blaire had smashed her sandal against a centipede.

My scalp prickled. I shot out of bed and moved through the thick air to the bathroom, where I drenched a washcloth under cold water, wrung it out and pressed it against my forehead like I had a fever. What kind of person hung out at a mall with the sole intention of kidnapping children?

I stayed awake for what felt like hours, my legs flopping all over the sheets. I got up and doused the washcloth again with cold water, laying it on different parts of my skin until finally, desperate for relief, I sucked out the water, hoping for a coolness to wash over me, but nothing worked.

Chapter 3

"I'VE BEEN THINKING," Mom said to us as we sat down to dinner. She wore a sleeveless white blouse with a big rounded collar, a light brown linen work skirt that went to her knees, and brown heels the color of a Hershey bar. She'd made tuna from the can, green beans and carrot salad with a Dijon vinaigrette. It was a good meal—one of her only meals—but I missed Dad's greasy steak and potatoes and his grilled peppers and onions.

"About what?" I couldn't get the newspaper sketch out of my mind. The *Post* reported that the guy with the closely set eyes and the disgusting dainty mustache was seen talking to the girls the day they disappeared.

Mom cleared her throat. "I know it'll sound sudden but…"

I slid my mood ring up to my knuckle and back down again, then did it over and over. "But what?"

"We need to sell the house."

"What?" Blaire's fork fell from her grasp and clanked against her plate.

"We could use the money, and a move would be good for us, I think," Mom went on, obviously giving us a speech she'd practiced. Probably with Aunt Julie.

"Move where?" I said.

"Wisconsin. Where Julie lives. To start over."

"Start *over*?" Blaire said, her voice rising. "Why do we need to start over?"

My fingers found each other and started to pick at loose skin around my nails.

Mom inhaled deeply and blew out her breath, which she'd been doing a lot lately. A balloon slowly deflating.

"Let's face it," she said. "We can't live in this house without your father. Everywhere we turn. Everything we do...and knowing that he's not..." Her hand went to her chest and I wondered if she was counting her heart beats like I'd started to do. She shook her head and her hair bounced. "I can't do it. I just can't do it anymore."

"I'm not leaving Danny," Blaire said, biting the side of her thumb. "You can't make me."

Our house was where Dad lived. Where we all lived together. Where he taught us how to knead dough and how to slice potatoes super thin and fry them in a pan with oil and salt. Dad was in the woodwork. We couldn't just leave him.

"You girls would have your own rooms," Mom said, hopeful. "Houses are a lot less expensive out there."

"Mom," I started, pulling a thread off my cut-offs. I knew what I wanted to say—scream, actually: *I'm not leaving!*—but nothing came out. I'd never yelled at her. That was Blaire's job.

"Don't try to bribe us!" Blaire yelled. "We're not going! *I'm* not going!" Her face turned splotchy, the blue veins in her temples clear as a road map.

The two of them locked eyes and, for a crazy second, I half-thought that Blaire was about to pick up her glass of milk and throw it at Mom. Or vice versa. But ever since Dad had died, it seemed like Mom had given Blaire permission to act however she wanted, no matter how rude.

Neither threw a glass; Blaire bolted from her seat and ran upstairs. Our bedroom door slammed and I knew she was facedown on the bed, tears soaking into her pillow like one big dark cloud.

I turned to Mom. Her lipstick had worn off even though she'd barely eaten. Her chin dropped to her chest like she couldn't bear to hold it up for one more second.

Outside, Arlo, the big dog down the street, barked. Beyond that, the crickets hummed.

"It'll be okay," I told her, awkwardly placing my hand on her back. Some people just knew what to do in those moments. Robin's mom would say something like, "Aw honey, everything'll turn out. Just you wait." In our case, though, things wouldn't turn out all right, especially now, since Mom wanted to move us halfway across the country. If only I were strong enough to yell at her and convince her that moving was a stupid idea, then maybe we could stay where we belonged. One day I'd stand up to her. But for now, I kept my words safe inside me, alongside my pounding heart.

Chapter 4

THE POLICE HELD a televised press conference to update the public about the Hanley case. I stood in the kitchen, glued to the T.V.

"Specially trained dogs have combed through fields and creeks," the balding police chief said, his voice deepening as his mouth found its way to the microphone. "Officers are searching storm drains and sewers. We're doing all we can."

I didn't get how they could check all those places and be so certain that the dogs didn't miss a key personal item, like one of the girls' barrettes or a tube of lip gloss.

The officer said what they needed the most was help from the public.

"If you were at the mall that day and saw anything that you think could help us…"

I exhaled, not even realizing I'd been holding my breath.

Mom left for Wisconsin and returned home on a record hot day, wearing large pearl earrings like the ones John Dean's wife wore during the televised Watergate hearings last year. Every time the camera focused on her, Mom would shake her head and say, "What a shame."

"What's a shame?" I remember asking her.

"That her husband dragged her through this. All because of Nixon."

But Dad stood firm. "Richard Nixon's a good man."

In Mom's hand was a bag of Chinese food that she'd picked up on the way home.

Usually we ordered egg rolls, wonton soup and sweet and sour pork. Today when I opened the cartons I saw chicken with broccoli and beef with peapods. Maybe the people at the restaurant gave Mom the wrong bag.

"No sweet and sour pork?" I asked Mom who clanked around in the utensil drawer.

"I thought we'd try something different."

I grabbed the fortune cookies at the bottom of the bag and tossed them on the table like dice. I grabbed one and split it open. *You will have pleasant surprise.*

When we sat down to eat, Mom sipped her glass of Soave Bolla and described a house smack dab on Lake Michigan that Julie had helped her find.

"Oh, and this'll interest you." She reached for her purse and fished around in it for something. "A witch lives down the street."

"I'm staying with Danny," Blaire said, her fingers making tiny shreds in her napkin. "He already asked his parents and they're fine with it."

"Wait," I said. "A witch?" I helped myself to chicken. I felt guilty for having an appetite, like it was proof that I didn't love Dad as much. That wasn't the case—I just wasn't as emotional.

"Some kooky woman," Mom said. "They call her the witch. Oh here it is." Between her fingers was a polaroid picture. I grabbed it, nearly dropping it right in the opened carton of beef.

A big white house with black shutters and lots of windows. A half circle driveway. The lake in the background. I showed it to Blaire, but she put up her hand like, Nope. Not looking.

"How can we afford this?" I said.

"We can." Mom nodded. "I've done the numbers. Plus, with the money your grandparents left me…"

"What money?"

"When they died."

I squinted. I hadn't known anything about extra money lying around. Mom always acted like we didn't have enough.

"Dad would never do this to us!" The vein in Blaire's neck bulged like a bubble about to burst.

Mom pressed her lips together. "Actually, that's not true." She slid her wine glass over an inch like we were playing Parcheesi and it was her turn. "Your father and I had discussed moving more than once. You know how unhappy he was at his job."

"Because he was an artist," Blaire threw back at Mom. "He couldn't stand to work in some stupid government office all day. I don't blame him."

"Yes, well." Her fingertips swept invisible crumbs from the table. She was biting her tongue, I could tell, but then an idea must've swooped down on her because for just a second she looked hopeful. "You know what this is? It's an opportunity. That's how we need to look at it." She tucked the picture back inside her purse and zipped it closed like the deal was done.

I remained focused on the fact that neither of them had helped themselves to the food.

Blaire rose so suddenly that her chair tipped back and fell to the kitchen floor, causing my heart to skip a beat and a ripple to skid across the surface of my milk. "You hated him, didn't you? Why don't you just admit it? *You* made him go back to work! *You* didn't let him do what he wanted to do! That's exactly why he died!"

"Blaire, don't," I said, stuffing another bite of chicken in my mouth.

"You think it's easy for me?" Mom said, her voice rising to Blaire's level. "You think I want to start my life over?"

"Go if you want," Blaire said, storming out of the room without retrieving her fallen chair. "I'm staying here."

Mom sighed.

The smell of wine drifted over to me and I wondered if I could get drunk from breathing it in. Maybe it would help me make sense of the rage that bounced back and forth between the two of them.

I grabbed at a fortune cookie and ripped off the plastic. My fingers trembled as I broke the cookie in half and pulled out the fortune. *The most important part in communication is listen to what not said.*

"We need to do *some*thing," Mom said to me. "We can't stay here. We just *can't.*"

The lump in my throat swelled up like a bee sting. I turned away, hiding my tears by squinting way into the dining room where I could just barely make out the framed photos on the mantle: Blaire pushing me on a swing; me hamming it up at the beach in a horrid yellow one piece; Dad in a red Santa hat, shoveling snow; Mom and Dad dressed up for Nixon's inaugural party.

True, quitting his job probably wasn't the smartest thing in the world, but I'd never forget the way he waltzed into the door that October night only six months ago, flipping on the kitchen radio and grabbing Mom from the stove and spinning her across the linoleum floor like Fred Astaire. She'd laughed, saying, "Did you get a raise or something?" and that was when he dipped her backwards and said, "Even better. I quit."

"What about the Mustang?" I asked her now. Dad's car had been sitting in the garage for months. As far as I knew, Mom hadn't driven it once.

"I don't know, honey. I hadn't thought of that."

"Can we take it with us?"

So I didn't come right out and say, "Actually, yes! Let's move!"; what I did was nod quickly, mostly so that Blaire—even though she was all the way upstairs—wouldn't hear me agree with Mom, but also to let Mom know that I was with her; I'd stay on her team. I had to. There was nowhere else to go.

"You're resilient," she told me. "That's a good quality to have."

Resilient. It sounded like a perfume. I liked that word. And finally I had something that Blaire didn't.

⚞⚟

Blaire screamed in her sleep the way she'd done after Dad had died. A horrible yelp that sent my heart into overdrive. I raced to her bed.

"It's okay, it's okay," I said in the dark.

"I can't leave him!" she sobbed.

Mom rushed in, wearing her fluffy yellow bathrobe that reminded me of a baby chick. "Blaire," she tried in a soft yet slightly alarmed tone. "I promise you'll be—"

"Get away from me!" She kicked her legs and Mom jerked away.

"Go!" Blaire went on. "I mean it!"

Mom rose, rushing out of the room and leaving us alone in the dark where Blaire continued to cry, and I sat, crouched by her bed, silently reciting heart attack facts. *Pain, fullness, and/or squeezing sensation of the chest; jaw pain, toothache, headache.*

"I'll die without him," she said. "I swear to God. I'll—"

"We'll visit," I tried, picking at a snag in her sheet. *Arm pain; upper back pain; general malaise.*

"We're *moving!*" she screamed at me. "Don't you get it?"

Her crying was never just a tear rolling down her cheek; hers was a hurricane, threatening to tear apart everything in its wake. Like Mom, I had no idea how to deal with it.

Shortness of breath; nausea; vomiting; sweating. When I reached the end of the list, I circled back to the top and, in my head, recited the symptoms again and again until the crying subsided and the steady sound of her breath going in and out lulled me back to sleep.

Chapter 5

A BIG BLUE basket leaned against the front door of our new house.

"Welcome to Milwaukee!" screamed the card. "Love, Aunt Julie."

Like ten different Wisconsin cheeses would erase the fact that we'd moved. It was so Julie. She thought food could fix everything. I moved the crackers and popcorn out of the way to see what else she'd given us. A paperback book peeked out called *Fun Facts About America's Dairyland*. Sounded riveting.

Mom fit the key in the lock and turned. Blaire trailed behind me, her Dr. Scholl's dragging against the stone walkway.

"Voila!" Mom pushed open the door like a game show hostess, pointing to the prizes we'd won.

I stepped in the front hallway and it creaked under my flip flops.

The house was all wood and angles and windows that looked out onto a vast green yard and, beyond that, Lake Michigan, which was much bigger than the oversized pond I'd imagined. The lake was bigger than life. It sparkled like gold. I couldn't believe we were hundreds of miles away from our house and street and Robin and everything else that made me who I was.

Blaire disappeared up the red, carpeted stairs and Mom drifted toward the bay window in her paper thin peach summer dress, her loose bun windblown from the drive. "It's perfect, isn't it?" She stood there, gazing at the late afternoon sun on the water. Maybe moving *was* a good thing. Maybe it was what you were supposed to do after your dad died—leave the memories and start a new life. Empty one house and fill another.

I went to the kitchen. Julie's basket sat on top of a moving box. I plucked out the fact book. *Cheese Facts* one chapter was titled. *Polish and German Settlers*.

My palm pressed against my chest. Seventy heart beats per minute. Which was seven beats higher than two hours ago. I'd die in Wisconsin, I just knew it. My pounding heart would shoot through my chest, spewing pieces of wet tissue all over our new house like confetti.

"Mom?" I said, reaching for the back of a chair.

Silence except for the sound of moving tape being ripped off a box.

I spread my fingers wide against my chest, then clutched it. "I think I'm having a heart attack."

"I can't hear you," she called in a singsong way.

Vrrrp. More tape pulled from seams.

"I'm…"

Snippets of Dad flashed in front of me—the sun spots on his temples and the paint specks in his hair. I saw him in the middle of our backyard saying, "First one to rake up a bag of leaves gets a hot fudge sundae!"

The minister at the funeral mentioned how the spirit of the loved one "surrounds the living," but what happened when you moved 770 miles away?

I picked up the phone on the wall, which was the kind of murky yellow-green that Robin would describe as "putrid." The dial tone blared like a car horn, screaming with urgency. I hid in the hallway so Mom couldn't see me and, without a thought about long distance costs, I dialed our old number.

After two rings, a woman answered. "Hello?"

Then someone else picked up—a girl who sounded about my age. "Hello?"

I listened to their silence, wondering where they were in the house.

"Hello?" the mother said in a worried tone.

"Hello?" the girl said, mimicking the mom.

"I guess it's no one," the girl said.

"Okay, hang up now, Sarah."

"They're still on," Sarah said.

I picked the bedroom that was closest to the stairs. Mom was right—we had more room, but it was weird not sharing a room with Blaire. I never thought I'd miss her silence and moodiness and her clothes all over the place.

At some point I fell asleep and woke in the morning missing our Maryland house so badly my stomach hurt.

I dressed in jean shorts and a halter top that I'd made out of a bandana and a shoe lace, and went to Mom's room, which was way too neat, like we'd been living in the house way longer than eighteen hours. She must've been up all night, trying to erase Maryland from her mind. On top of her sheets was the light green blanket with the thin satin strip going down the middle that I used to rub my finger against when I was little. Her bedside table held all the same items that occupied her Maryland bedside table—face cream, Kleenex, a bottle of aspirin.

I turned away and headed to Blaire's room, where half-opened moving boxes littered her carpet. I didn't get how she lived in such a mess all the time. Once I found a mug under her desk with a tea bag totally hardened to the bottom.

She sat cross-legged on her bed, writing furiously, a box of stationery on her lap. Already she'd tacked up Dannyland, but the light didn't stretch all the way to the photos like it did in our Maryland house, so in some pictures Danny's eyes appeared darker than they were, making him look almost sinister.

"It's an hour later in Maryland right now," I told her.

"No shit, Sherlock."

"I'm just telling you. *God*. What's your problem?"

She kept scribbling, her pen barely lifting from the paper. Her hair was unbrushed and thrown back in a loose braid that she'd probably slept in.

"You're not the only one who's not thrilled about moving, you know," I said.

She glared at me. "It's not just the move, you idiot." She folded a letter, slid her tongue across the seal of the envelope and took out a new sheet of stationery.

"You mean Dad?"

She shook her head. "Just forget it."

I hated when she said "Just forget it." That and "Nothing" when I asked her to repeat something. Like I was supposed to read her mind.

"You mean Danny?" I guessed.

That time she didn't even use words. She flicked her hand like I was an annoying mosquito.

"Fine. I don't even *care*." And I left in a huff, thinking, Why can't she be more resilient?

Mom stood in the middle of the kitchen, wearing a blue linen skirt and a white sleeveless blouse. She ate the last spoonfuls of cottage cheese, her spoon clanking against the glass bowl.

Spread out on the table was a map that, at the top, said, *Milwaukee's North Shore*.

"We're right here," she said, pointing at a red dot.

I didn't care where we were. I wanted to be in Maryland.

"This area over here is where I'd really like to focus." Her new job with Moyer Real Estate would start the same day we started school.

She tapped her nail on another spot. "But this is where the real money is." She squinted as if she could just barely make out hundred dollar bills floating in the air.

"How'd you sleep?" she asked.

I shrugged and went to the fridge. "Fine."

"I slept like a baby," she said, smiling at the memory. "First time in months. Slept right through the night." She looked pretty and fresh, not at all like a wife whose husband had recently died.

"The lake air is nice, isn't it?" she said, hopeful. "The nice fresh air coming through the window?"

I resented her good mood. Plus you didn't just leave the house you'd lived in forever because you couldn't "take it anymore."

"Do we have anything to eat?"

"Make an egg drink."

Milk, an egg, and a sprinkle of chocolate Quik or Sanka grounds for flavoring. Put it all in a blender and it's "the perfect meal." She expected me to love it like she did, but I hated egg drink.

"Is there cereal anywhere?"

She pointed to a cabinet and I felt her watching me take out the blue bowl and the box of Raisin Bran. She smiled a little, like she had a secret she couldn't wait to share.

"What?" I said.

"Tell me you aren't just the teensiest bit excited about this move." Her brows rose in a hopeful way. "Just a teensy bit?"

It was how she talked when we were little. "How 'bout a teensie tiny bit of soup?" when we were sick. Even "teensie weensie." I wondered if living in Wisconsin would bring back that part of her that always made me feel warm and cozy, not like now, where I felt like the rug had been pulled out from under me.

"How can you be happy?" I said.

Her eyes narrowed and the smile melted away, causing a bolt of guilt to rip through me.

"You think I'm happy?" she said.

I backed off, fearing an argument. "No, it's just…"

She did the balloon sigh, then reached for the coffee pot. "You know what I decided this morning?"

Before I could say, "What?" she said, "I decided that I have to pretend that he's on a trip. A long trip." She poured dark coffee in her mug.

"Dad?"

She nodded, flipping on the faucet. "It's the only way I can get through this—by thinking he'll be back."

I had no idea that adults did that kind of thing. Pretended things. Lied to themselves. I couldn't figure out if it was a good or bad thing to do. I wondered if any of us would get back to normal or if Dad's dying had permanently changed us all, but in different ways. I had the heart palpitations; Blaire was pissed all the time; and now Mom had taken up lying to herself.

Outside a car honked twice.

"Who's that?" I said.

"Must be Julie." Her foot stepped in the direction of the honk, then she turned around and peered into my eyes. "I loved your father. You know that, right?"

Yes, I did know that, but I wanted her to be miserable and confused like she'd been before we moved. I wanted her to start spacing out in the car again because that would mean that Wisconsin hadn't erased the memory of him.

"I think about him all the time," she said. Her eyes turned a lighter green as they filled with tears.

"Right here," she whispered, placing her palm against her chest and spreading out her fingers like a fan. "This whole area. Sometimes it's so heavy I can't breathe."

I had the opposite of heaviness. I worried that the smallest wind could pick me up and throw me in a dark hole forever.

"Come on," she said. "Let's go see Julie."

In the driveway we watched as she parked her bright blue convertible. She and Dad had a thing about old cars. The gasoline smell reminded me so much of our Mustang that I could practically feel the black vinyl seats sticking to my bare thighs. I could see Blaire and me in the back, laughing, our hair blowing wildly, and Dad up front, behind dark sunglasses, shaking his head, saying, "My two hyenas."

"When's the Mustang getting here?" I asked Mom.

She put up her hand to shield the sun. "Maybe a month or so."

"'A *month* or so?' Why does it take so long?"

"I don't know, honey. It just does."

Julie emerged from her car. Her long dark hair was streaked with wiry grey strands that didn't lie flat. You could tell that she and Dad were from the same family, but when you put them next to each other, it was hard to pinpoint exactly what was the same. Their love for food, of course, but you couldn't exactly see that unless you focused on the extra padding around their waists.

"*So* glad you're here," she said, throwing her thick arms around Mom, who seemed smaller and almost concave next to Julie.

When Mom broke free of the hug, Julie turned to me, her head tilted in that "Poor Martie" way that made me feel both swallowed up and deeply loved. Her arms opened up like a bird's wings getting ready to swoop down on its prey, and my calves stiffened, bracing for one of her suffocating hugs.

It turned out to be not that bad. It was actually kind of nice. Julie was all flesh as opposed to Mom's boniness and I wanted to close my eyes and just be held in her softness for a while.

After we let go, she said, "Boy, we need to fatten you both up, don't we? Get you some nice grilled bratwurst."

I glanced at Mom like, Bratwurst? What? And Julie said, "Sausages. Polish sausages. On the grill? On a summer day? Nothing like it."

She peered way into my eyes and said, "So how *are* you?" She pronounced "are" like "air." She was a high school counselor and loved hearing about people's problems. But I didn't have problems. I was the one who kept things together, the one who didn't make waves. The easy one. Mom's favorite.

"I'm fine…I mean…" I stammered, searching the clogged corners of my brain for something deep to say, realizing for the first time that maybe it wasn't such a great idea to be so closed up.

Julie nodded at me like, *It's okay. I get it: You still have no idea how to show your emotions.* She squeezed my shoulder. "I'm here if you need me."

I nodded. "Okay."

She turned to Mom and, with wide, excited eyes, said, "Did you hear? He's been ordered to hand over the tapes."

"What?" Mom said, her hand blocking the sun.

"Nixon. The tapes. The Supreme Court just ruled it."

"Oh. I haven't been…"

"So now we'll get the real story." Julie winked at me like I was as much of a Nixon hater as she was. I didn't *hate* him, mostly because Dad liked him so much, but I didn't trust him, either.

Mom waved her hand and a waft of Norell perfume drifted my way. "Come inside. It's still a mess, but…"

They went into the living room, where yesterday she'd instructed the movers where to place the furniture, and now she and Julie sat on the worn rose-colored couch, their voices hushed, quiet as mice. If only I could read lips. Why couldn't they talk in normal voices?

I drifted upstairs, wondering if Robin was as lonely as I was. It was probably worse for her since she was stuck in a foreign country.

I picked up the hall phone and called our old house again.

"Who?" Sarah, the girl who now lived there, said. "Martie *who*?"

"I used to live there. You bought the house from us." I pulled the long twirly cord into the bathroom that Blaire and I shared.

"You're the one whose dad died, right?" she said.

I closed the door. "How'd you know that?"

"My mom told me."

"How'd *she* know?" I glanced at my reflection. Startled eyes, worried mouth.

"The real estate person told her, I think."

"Wait. Why was the real estate person talking about my dad?"

"I don't know. I *thought* it was your dad. Maybe I'm wrong."

What was her problem? *Maybe* it was my dad?

I peered into an opened moving box that no one had unpacked—Herbal Essence shampoo, Vaseline, Midol, an eyelash curler, white towels, and the washcloth that in Maryland I'd doused in cold water and pressed across my forehead.

"What room are you in right now?" I asked her.

"Why do you care?"

"I know a lot of secrets about that house." I took the items out of the box and placed them on the shelves. Mom had never talked to us about our periods like Robin's mom had with her. I didn't even know how she actually knew I'd gotten mine, but every few months, packages of Stayfree Mini Pads and boxes of Tampax silently appeared in the bathroom closet like we all were in on the secret, but no one spoke about it.

"Like what kind of secrets?" Sarah asked.

I closed the door. "Just stuff." There weren't any secrets—at least none that I knew about—but I wanted her to know that, although her family now inhabited the house, I'd always know more about it than she ever would.

"We think our house in California was nicer," she said. "This one's too old."

"It has character," I said, wondering if we'd left anything behind—an old tube of Clearasil? One of Dad's paintbrushes? After the funeral, Mom had made several trips to Goodwill, dropping off most of Dad's clothes and all the trinkets and "junk" on his bureau. Junk like cufflinks and business cards. She said it was easier to get rid of things than to keep them because we didn't want to accumulate clutter, which made no sense because it wasn't like we were adding clutter. Dad's stuff had always been there. But she wanted it gone. All of it.

"Why don't people have pools here?" Sarah asked me.

"Some people do. If you want one, you could probably just build it." I noticed water leaking around the faucet. I ripped off a few squares of toilet paper and soaked it up, but after a few seconds, it returned, pooling around the faucets. Leaks already. That wasn't a good sign.

"The backyard's like a foot long," Sarah said.

I threw the wet toilet paper in the toilet. "Why'd you buy the house if you hate it so much?"

The connection got all crackly and I worried that I'd lost her. "Hello? Hello?"

"I need to go. I've got piano."

"Wait!" I was gripping the phone so hard that my hand actually hurt. "Any news about the Hanley sisters?"

"You didn't hear?"

"Hear what? Did something happen?" I closed the cabinet door, but instead of latching, it swung open.

"Dead," Sarah said.

My stomach dropped. "Are you serious?"

"Uh huh."

Ever since their disappearance, I'd skimmed the paper every single day, but now that we were in Wisconsin, I hadn't seen the newspaper. I never thought I'd actually miss major news like that.

"When did it happen?" I said, sinking. "How is this possible?"

"Last week. The guy chopped them up into little pieces."

My eyes closed. All of my worst fears about them had come true. I slumped on the bathroom floor, which was cool against the back of my thighs. I wanted to cry, but nothing came out.

"You there?" she said.

The back of my throat quivered. I barely got out an "Mm."

"Wow," she said. "You're easy to fool."

"What?"

She laughed. "I just wanted to see if you'd believe me."

My thumb and index finger pinched the bridge of my nose the way Mom did when she was trying to help me with Math homework.

"Wait," I said. "You're *joking* about them?"

"Don't freak out. It's not a big deal."

I stood and slammed the cabinet. That time it latched. "I can't be*lieve* you'd lie about them!"

"God! Don't have a conniption fit!"

"I'll do whatever I want!"

In a fury, I flew down the stairs and at the bottom, I heard Julie say, "You're doing really well," like Mom was a toddler who'd taken a tiny step without falling. "You are."

"I'm not," Mom countered. "For one, I can't handle Blaire any-more. I really can't. And Martie—she's constantly..." And her voice faded. Of course. Right at the most crucial part. I was constantly *what*? Constantly a pain in the butt? Constantly thinking I was having a heart attack?

The back screen door was stuck, but I forced it open, nearly ripping out the screen. I didn't care. I hated the house. And I hated Mom for saying she couldn't deal with us. Blaire I could understand, but me? What was *I* doing that she couldn't handle?

I marched toward the lake, my bare soles meeting the cool Milwaukee grass. The air was clear and the sky was blue and I found myself longing for a steamy Maryland day, the kind I used to complain about.

Five rickety steps at the edge of our lawn led to a small patch of sand. The water crept forward and back like the ocean. It stretched all the way to my toes. Freezing. So freezing it burned. I couldn't believe Sarah had lied about the girls. What was wrong with her?

I stepped back and my foot almost landed on two silver fish that had washed ashore. Ale wives. I'd read about them yesterday in that stupid fact book. I grabbed a stick and flung them in the water. Yuck.

I went back up the steps and parked myself in one of the four white patio chairs that Mom had already put on the lawn. Four because we were once a family of four. Three was a horrible number. A lonely number. On spring breaks in Florida, Dad and Blaire paired up, swimming way out in the ocean while Mom and I clung to the safety of the pool, our shoulders and noses slathered with Sea and Ski. How would we split up now? Me and Blaire on one team and Mom all alone on the other? No. We were three teams now, each of us floating alone.

I closed my eyes and tilted my face to the sun.

"Oh yeah, the tan one," I wanted people at my new school to say. "I like her." No. That was Blaire. She tanned; I burned.

A shadow made me open my eyes. That and the smell of vanilla lip smacker.

Blaire held a stack of stamped envelopes in one hand. I thought she'd plunk on the grass, but she just stood there, squinting at the lake. I did, too. It was hypnotic. My eyes went from one section of the lake to another and then all the parts bled together.

"I'm going to that witch's house," she said.

My hand went to my forehead to block the sun. "I don't think that's a very good idea."

"Oh, okay, Mom." She knew that would bug me.

"She could put a curse on you," I called to her as she started to walk away.

"Good," she said. "I hope she does."

Chapter 6

THE WITCH'S HOUSE was small as a cottage and covered in vines. Besides the overgrown grass and weeds, bizarre human-like wood sculptures filled the yard. And figures made out of stones. Mobiles dangled from tree branches.

Near the front door was a huge face with gnarled driftwood for hair and, right next to it: a life-sized sculpture of someone about my height made out of sticks.

Suspicious, I turned around quickly, certain someone was about to grab me. I just knew that the witch was watching us from a window, deciding whom to take first.

"Dad would love this," Blaire said, lacing her fingers around the chain link fence that separated us from the yard.

It was true. He'd pull over and get out of the car. He'd probably talk to the witch, too, say something like, "So tell me about this face over here," and be genuinely interested and not one bit scared. I didn't get what made them both so intrigued and me so scared.

I tilted back my head to take in the summer sky, but instead a mobile swinging from a tree branch blocked my view—a crescent-shape holding three people—two small, one big.

I turned away and a face constructed of tiny stones stared at me.

"Let's go," I said, but Blaire's eyes went from piece to piece like she was taking a mental snapshot of each one.

"This is incredible."

Incredible was a firework that zoomed up to the sky and broke open like the most amazing flower you'd ever seen. Incredible was a piece of homemade bread, fresh from the oven, with butter melting on top. It was not a yard filled with rocks and stones and faces that stared at you like, *Well?* no matter where you stood.

"So when do tryouts start?" I asked, trying to lure her away from the house.

When she didn't answer, I pushed on. "You think people will be good here? At tennis? Or better in Maryland?"

She glared at me. "I don't know, Martie. Why don't you take a survey?"

"What's your problem?"

The sun hit her eyes and for a second they looked like marbles, swirling in the light. "Nothing."

Finally she turned away from the fence and we went down to a strip of narrow beach where a hollowed-out log laid on its side, flies buzzing on one end. The air was cool and hot at the same time.

We sat on a huge flat slab of rock, which warmed my legs. I couldn't get over the size of the lake. Waves rolled onto the wet sand, creeping toward us.

"You know what I don't get?" I tossed a rock toward the water, but it bounced off a bigger rock and disappeared in a crevice. "I don't get how a heart just stops."

Even though I'd read the section on heart attacks in the *Merck Manual* about twenty times, nothing made sense.

"Seriously," I said. "How does a perfectly healthy heart just stop like that?"

"Who says his heart was healthy?"

I turned around. Already Blaire's nose and cheeks were pink from the sun. Pink that would turn golden brown, making her teeth appear even whiter.

"We would've known if something was wrong with him," I said.

She shrugged with one shoulder.

"If he had heart disease, we would've known it," I said, lining up a row of small stones I'd gathered.

"Yeah, but does it matter? It's all the same: He's gone. Forever."

Certain words made it all too real. Like *forever.* That one hit me like a punch in the gut.

"And he's never coming back," she said.

I took one of those huge breaths that Mom had become famous for lately and now I understood why she did it—because it was like someone had stolen all your air and you were just trying to get a little bit back.

A cool breeze blew part of my hair into my face and I pushed it away. "You still have his ashes?"

"What do you think? I threw them out?"

"I never said you did! God!" I stood and attempted to walk away from her, but after a few steps, the rocks under my flip flops teetered and I just knew I'd fall and break my leg before the first day of school, so I stayed on a tippy one and positioned my feet on opposite ends so that I could balance.

I hated that Dad had been cremated. I wanted to see his face one last time.

"No, you don't," Mom had said. "The way those funeral people put makeup on the person—it's not the way you want to remember him. Believe me."

"I *hate* her!" Blaire said, startling me for a second. "It's all her fault!" She hurled a stone way out in the water and it went *plunk!*

If empty had a sound, that was it: *Plunk.* A vanishing. A sudden disappearance.

In early August, I got a letter from Robin saying that she and her family were staying in Singapore for two years. "Can you be*lieve* it?" she'd scribbled on scented stationery. "They knew the *entire* time and just didn't want to tell us."

I wrote her back immediately, saying how unfair it was. Secretly I was glad we were both miserable.

Two weeks before school started, Nixon admitted that he'd withheld information about the Watergate break-in and, three days later, he resigned.

Mom sat in the living room in her summer dress and sandals, glued to the T.V.

Seated at a desk with phony blue curtains in back of him, Nixon looked stiff and uncomfortable as he read from a small stack of papers. He said he'd never been a quitter. He said that he thought his "wrongdoings" had been in the best interest of the country.

"*Wrong*doings?" I said to the T.V. "You mean lying?"

"Shh," Mom said.

David Brinkley said it was a historic day. Everyone kept saying that. All I kept thinking was, The leader of our country lied. To everyone. Wasn't that the main point?

"So what happens now?" I asked Mom. Were those tears in her eyes?

"Well, the vice president steps in now."

"Is that good or bad?"

"Neither. It's just a sad day."

That made no sense. "I thought you hated Nixon."

She turned to me like I'd deeply offended her. "I've never 'hated' him. He did a lot for this country."

"Like what? Like, make everyone mistrustful?"

The next day he stood at a podium. You could see the sweat on his upper lip. He kept clearing his throat and I couldn't figure out if he was trying to hold back tears or not.

One of his daughters had blonde, shiny hair like a Breck girl.

The camera followed the family as they walked toward the helicopter. The daughter's hair blew all over the place.

Mom wiped her eyes.

As Nixon did his famous two-handed peace wave, the camera zoomed in on his face and I studied it, trying to figure out how Dad could've liked such a surly person.

"It is indeed the end of an era," someone else said for the fiftieth time.

Chapter 7

ON THE MORNING of the first day of school, I read the *Merck Manual* while trying to force down a few bites of Corn Chex, but the milk was cold against my teeth and my stomach kept flopping like I was on a roller coaster. *A person experiencing a heart attack may not even be sure of what is happening. Many heart attacks start slowly, unlike the dramatic portrayal often seen in the movies.*

Maybe Dad had been having symptoms for a long time—years, even. And maybe that was the reason he'd been in the hospital with that weird virus. He stayed for a whole month. At least it seemed like a month. I was only seven, but I remember him being sick before he left—not with a fever—just sleeping a lot in their bedroom, the shades drawn. Mom kept saying, "Don't go in there. He's contagious."

When he returned home, he was thin and barely cracked a smile. Every morning I raced out the door after he left for work, yelling his name and shaking his pills over my head like maracas.

Clickclickclickclick. Mom's heels. I counted her footsteps. If I were anywhere in the world and heard those rushed heels, I'd know exactly who it was.

"Hi honey." Her perfume swept through the kitchen and fell on me lightly, like a shawl. She wore a fancy beige blouse and a black slim skirt that hugged her butt. Blow-dried hair, gold hoops. It was her first day at the job. She didn't seem nervous in the slightest bit.

"What are you…" Her head turned sideways as she read the spine of my book. "Oh. That." She pulled out the coffee pot, filled it partway with water and poured it into the coffee maker. Almost immediately the machine responded with a gurgle.

I wondered if anyone in Maryland missed me. Robin would be starting her new school in Singapore by now. And Matt Fleming would kiss someone new, maybe this time with his tongue. The Hanley sisters wouldn't be starting school like everyone else. Their lockers would remain empty, their names on the attendance list unchecked.

"A routine will be good for us," Mom said, taking out the blue and white mug that we bought one year in Williamsburg. She moved across the kitchen in short, quick steps, grabbing the milk from the fridge and ending up at the counter by the window, watching the dark drips of coffee slowly fill the glass pot.

"Do you know anything about the people who bought our house?" I asked.

Mom poured the coffee and the steam swirled up like smoke from a cigarette. She added a splash of skim milk. Blue milk, Blaire and I called it.

"A family from California. California or Florida. Somewhere warm." She fanned her face. "Woo! Hot in here."

It wasn't, but Mom had been getting hot flashes lately.

"Did that virus have anything to do with Dad's heart attack?" I asked her.

"What virus?"

"When he was in the hospital."

It was weird, like her brain had a sudden power outage. She just sort of stared at me for a second. Maybe a result of all the months of not sleeping? But she'd been sleeping like a baby now that we'd left Maryland. When her brain lights came back on, she flipped off the coffee maker and said, "Why aren't you eating?"

I looked down at my abandoned cereal. The pieces floated like tiny rafts, softening and shredding. *You can lower your chances of heart attack by treating conditions that make a heart attack more likely, such as high blood cholesterol and high blood pressure.*

"Did he have high blood pressure?" I asked, twirling my ring and then pulling it up over my knuckle.

"No."

"Heart disease?"

Mom wet a sponge and dragged it across the counter. "I think that book is putting some crazy ideas in your head."

"No it isn't," I said. "I'm just trying to find out what went wrong."

"Yes, I understand that." She let crumbs fall into her cupped hand. "But sometimes a heart just stops."

The school bus smelled like spilled milk and detergent. Blaire sat across from me, writing a letter to Danny and doodling in the margins, drawing a series of lines that connected with other lines. Like branches. Or lightning bolts.

She wore Levis that were faded exactly the right amount, a flowy white top and a silver chain with the floating heart that Danny had given her. My hair was pulled back in a pathetic ponytail because I couldn't get it to look normal, and my blue shorts and yellow Lacoste shirt that Mom had picked up from a thrift store were all wrong. Not to mention my forehead, where a spray of pimples had flared up yesterday, just in time to meet new people.

At the dead end, near the witch's house, a pretty blonde girl wearing a tight purple shirt trotted up the steps. She glanced at me and I smiled at her, hopeful, but she sauntered past me like she had better things to do than talk to a zitty new girl.

At lunch, I sat with Allie, a girl with short dark hair like a boy's and a perfectly round mole under her left eye.

"So have you seen the lake yet?" She wore white shorts and a royal blue warm up jacket with a white stripe down the side.

"The lake?" I said. "Yeah, it's in our backyard."

She looked up. "Wait. You're on Beach Drive?" Her skin was creamy, like a doll's.

"Uh huh." I opened my lunch—bologna and iceberg lettuce on rye bread, a green apple and salted carrot sticks. I'd made the sandwich last night before bed and been so hungry that I'd taken a bite and now I wished I hadn't.

"Fan-*cee*. God." Allie pronounced it *Gahd*. "You must be rich."

I shook my head. "No," I said. "I mean…"

Actually, it was confusing. Mom had always acted like we were teetering on the edge of an empty bank account, but for three years now she'd had that money from her parents, enough to buy us a house on Lake Michigan. Why had she acted like we were so broke all the time?

"My brother, Tommy, once found a dog skull on the beach. Dogs die in the lake all the time—when it freezes, I mean. They slide in and can't get out." She shrugged. "All I've found are beer cans and used rubbers."

"Gross," I said though I wasn't sure how she knew the rubbers were used or not.

A scream rang out, rippling across the lunchroom.

"That's Shelly Stires," Allie said, rolling her eyes. "Right there. She's on swim team with me and my brother."

It was the girl who ignored me on the bus that morning. You could tell she was popular just by looking at her. Her blonde head was thrown back as she laughed and yelled, "Oh my God! That's *so* funny!"

"She's in love with Tommy. She lives near the witch."

I stopped chewing. "You know the witch?"

"God, yeah. Everyone does. Well, not *know*, but know *of*." She held out a small bag of potato chips. "Want some?"

My fingers dipped in and fished out a few.

"You know all those faces in her yard?" she said.

"Uh huh."

"People say each one represents people she's killed," Allie said.

I squinted. "What?"

"And if you get too close to her house, you'll turn to stone." She shrugged. "That's what I've been hearing since like first grade."

"Maybe her sister's the wicked witch of the west," I said, trying to lighten the rumors. Not only did the Hanley kidnapper freak me out, but now apparently Wisconsin had its own version—a serial killer who just happened to live down the street from us.

"Her family all died," Allie went on, crumbling up her empty bag. "That part's true. It was in the paper."

"What happened?"

"Her husband and two sons. No one knows. Their bodies were never found." She shrugged. "The big rumor is that she killed them and buried them under her front yard."

I rubbed the back of my neck.

"You probably don't have anything to worry about, though," she said.

"*Prob*ably?"

The bell rang. "I mean, it was just her family she wanted to kill. Not like, neighbors."

"You said she killed a bunch of people." I stood, grabbed my lunch bag, which felt sweaty in my grasp.

"Yeah, but not recently."

What did *that* mean? That the witch had lost interest in killing people? Was that supposed to make me feel better?

We tossed our paper bags in the trash can and joined the flow of students making their way out of the cafeteria while another set came streaming in. An ocean of unfamiliar faces. I'd bet fifty bucks that every single one had a father.

"You'll be fine," Allie said as she reached in her front pocket and took out a small container of Carmex. "Just don't go inside her house." With her pinky finger, she applied a dab to her lips and pressed them together the way my mom did after putting on lipstick. "Okay?"

Chapter 8

"I GOT THE phone bill," Mom said a week after school had started. We were in the basement, doing laundry. I sorted darks from whites while Mom sprayed stain remover on a few items, like the hem of Blaire's tennis shorts where maybe Coke had spilled. "Are you aware of someone calling our old number?"

My face warmed. Shit. I'd forgotten about the phone bill. "Our Maryland number?" I asked, stalling for time and playing dumb.

Mom didn't buy it. "Yes, Martie. Our Maryland number." She wore her no-nonsense weekend look—khaki pants, white button-down shirt, Tretorns. No makeup or earrings. She looked severe without the lipstick. She'd hate to hear it, but, without makeup, she looked like her own mom—our grandmother—who'd died three years ago. Mom only talked about her when she said things like, "She never held me. Not once. Can you imagine? Not holding your own daughter?"

"I just wanted to know who lived there," I admitted, stuffing the darks into the wash machine.

"And what did you find out?" *Cht cht.* She sprayed two pair of underwear, then let them drop in a pile by her feet where other stained items sat, soaking.

"Some girl and her parents." I measured a cup of light blue powdered detergent and shook it on top of the dark clothes. The lid dropped and the cycle began. "She was weird. She said the Hanley girls were dead."

"Oh dear God."

"You think they're still alive?" I asked her.

Mom's hair was pulled back with a large tortoise shell barrette, but a section had come free. Now that we were out of the humidity, her hair had lost its frizz and it lay limp, the one clump framing the left side of her face. "I don't know, Martie. I don't like thinking about that. It's a terrible story." She continued to spray. *Cht cht*

It wasn't like I loved thinking about the Hanley girls either, but I couldn't help it. They occupied the same part of my brain that Dad's death did—the unsettled region that seemed to be taking up more and more space every day.

I turned away and meandered around the cellar. It was like our Maryland one. Old and creepy. Spiders in the corner. Not all cozy with wall-to-wall carpet and beanbag chairs like at Robin's house. Every time I went up our stairs, I prayed a hand wouldn't grab my leg.

"It smells like a dead animal in here," I said, walking by the furnace.

"What?" she called over the rushing water. "Did you say 'dead animal'?"

On the weekends Dad painted in one of the small rooms near the laundry area. Mom always said, "Don't you want a couch or some chairs or *some*thing in here?" but he liked it bare, just a bulb overhead, a floor lamp, an easel and half-finished canvasses leaning against the walls.

Each painting was similar to the next—smears of red and blue, reckless arcs, mysterious specks of light. Layers upon layers of paint that made you want to travel inside the colors. Once I asked Blaire what the paintings meant and she snapped at me. "Does it matter, Martie? God! Do you have to have everything spelled out for you?" And when I asked why they were all so similar, she told me I wasn't deep enough to see the differences.

Maybe if I watched him for hours the way she did, mesmerized by each flick of the paintbrush, I'd get it.

"This place could use a face lift," Mom said, coming up behind me.

"Maybe you could wallpaper it."

She'd done that to our Maryland basement the day after Dad died. She'd needed to be alone, she told us, and that it helped to work with her hands.

I thought it was weird that she wasn't sobbing in her bed like Blaire or weeping quietly in the bathroom like me, but Julie assured me that everyone grieved in different ways and, if someone wanted to wallpaper a basement in the wake of a death, then that was exactly what that person needed to do.

"We should get a ping pong table," I said, feeling in my pocket for the Jolly Rancher I'd stuffed in there earlier.

Mom brought her arms in close to her waist. "It would be freezing down here in the winter, though." She glanced up at the ceiling and walls in a worried way, like it was a cave we were trapped inside and she'd just realized there was no way out.

"That girl in Maryland thinks our house is haunted," I said. "She goes, 'It has a weird vibe.' She actually said that—*vibe*."

Mom sniffed the air. "I don't smell anything in here."

"What happened to all of his paintings?" I asked, fearing that she'd tossed them in the trunk of her car and dropped them at Goodwill.

"Your father's? He got rid of most of them."

"Got *rid* of them?" That was definitely a lie. He wouldn't get rid of his own creations.

One shoulder shrugged as she glanced around the room. "You know how he was."

No, not really. I didn't know how he was. I was getting the feeling that he acted one way with Mom and another way with us.

"One day he'd be excited about a certain project," Mom said, "and the next day he'd paint right over it. Or throw it out." Her hand went to a crack in the wall, her fingertips tracing it all the way down to the baseboard.

"Did you save any of them?"

She looked at me like I'd said the most absurd thing. "Martie. You think he just put the canvas in the kitchen trashcan and that was that?"

"Well...." How was I supposed to know where he dumped the paintings?

"He'd tear them up with...I don't know...a knife, probably. Those paintings were far from salvageable."

The dead animal smell came alive again. "Wait. Smell that?" But then it vanished and all I smelled was the sharp promise of clean clothes.

"Well, I hope there's no dead animal," she said, heading for the stairs. "That's the last thing we need. Oh Martie, grab those sheets from the dryer, will you?"

I made a beeline for the laundry room, but as soon as I opened the dryer, the lights went out. Great.

"Mom!" I yelled. Out of habit, she must've accidentally flipped the switch. "I'm in the dark!"

"Oh! Sorry!" It was weird how completely dark it got. When the light returned, so did my imagination, screeching from one horrid Hanley sisters scenario to another. What if they'd been tied up in a dark basement all those months? My mind bounced back and forth, from "They're alive" to "They're definitely dead." I had to find out the latest news, *real* news. Not some disgusting lie about a guy chopping their bodies into tiny pieces. So what if the call cost three dollars? I'd pay for it.

Carrying the sheets, I raced up the cellar stairs past the kitchen where a male voice on the portable black and white T.V. said, "The man's a crook. We all know that."

"He's not a crook," Mom said to herself as she added a few spoonfuls of Sanka to the blender. "He's just a man who—" and the blender whirred.

It's the perfect meal!

She poured her frothy drink into a tall glass and said, "People aren't perfect."

"Nixon, you mean?"

"You know what I hope?" she said, sipping her egg drink. "I hope he's out there in California, sitting in the sun, not giving one more thought to everything that happened." She smiled in a dreamy way like she pictured herself right next to him, basking in the brightness.

I hadn't followed the case closely, but I kind of doubted that an impeached president would be hanging out, poolside, not thinking about the huge scandal he'd caused.

Once on the second floor, I went straight for the phone and dialed our old number.

After Sarah answered, I said, "You have to promise never to lie about the Hanley sisters again."

"Okay," she said. "Promise."

"On a stack of bibles?"

"On a stack of bibles."

"Okay." I stretched the cord into my room and closed the door. I sat, perched on the edge of my bed. "So is there any news?"

"Some lady thought she saw one of them in the back of a car."

I stood. "Really?"

"She was on the highway and looked over for a second and thought she saw them, but..."

"But what?" I scooted over to my desk where the Merck Manual was opened to a drawing of the heart.

"It wasn't them."

I sighed and turned away from the book. "Why can't they just find them? Why is this taking so long?"

"No one goes to that mall anymore. Everyone's still freaked out."

I paced around my small room, glancing at the contents on my bureau—the jug of Ten-O-Six, the overflowing pile of cotton balls, and my jewelry box where I'd displayed my liquid silver necklaces according to length.

"So you never told me the secrets about this house," she said.

"Oh." I smiled, pulling out my top drawer and grabbing the jar of ashes. "There's nothing, really. I was just kidding around." I unscrewed the top of the jar and dipped my fingertips inside. A residue stuck to my index finger and I wiped it on my leg, then felt guilty and weird that a part of him remained on my skin. What part was it? A fraction of his wrist bone? A shred of his heart?

"I know a secret," she said.

I screwed the top back on the jar and shimmied it between the socks.

"Well, it might not be that secret," she said. "Wanna guess?"

My brain scanned the nooks and crannies of our old house. "I know! The centipedes that come up from the bathroom drain and crawl around the tub."

"Guess again."

I squinted into the air. "Ahmmmmm." Secrets about the house? "Oh! I know."

"What?"

"The little room in the attic has a secret door."

"Close but no cigar."

I sighed, impatient. "What, then? Just tell me."

"It's about your dad."

"*My* dad? What about him?"

"You sure you don't want to keep guessing?"

"I'm sure." What could she possibly know about my dad?

"He killed himself in your basement."

My stomach dropped to my feet. "*What?*"

"My mom told me. She said your dad shot himself in the head."

"My dad had a heart attack!"

"Oh."

My heart raced. *Was* it true? Of course it wasn't true.

"I can't believe you even said that!" What was wrong with her? First she lied about the Hanley girls and now about my dad.

"Sorry. It must've been some other guy."

After I hung up, my mind frantically scanned each house on our old street, wondering with whom she could've gotten him confused, but I didn't know every single dad on that street. Shot himself in the head? What was she even thinking?

I took out my spiral notebook and turned to a fresh page. My heart pounded in my ears. My pen tip touched the light blue line. Who did she think she was, mistaking him for someone else? I threw the notebook aside and marched to the phone. "It's not true," I told her. "Someone has him confused with another dad."

I waited for her to say, "You're right. It wasn't your dad." Or "Wow, you're easy to fool." But she didn't say a thing. Maybe she was too embarrassed to speak.

"My dad would never do something like that." My voice trembled. "And I really don't appreciate you just assuming that it's the truth."

"God, alright, Martie. Cool your jets."

"You cool your jets!" I slammed down the phone, rushed to the bathroom and yanked on the faucet full blast and stood there, washing my hands over and over until my skin burned.

Water leaked from the base of the faucet, trickling out and pooling on the porcelain. I turned off the water, wiped my wet hands on my shorts and went to Blaire's room where, on her bed, she drew in a large sketch pad, her lips pursed. She looked so normal sitting there, like she wasn't processing some horrific lie that someone had told her. A Neil Young album played on her turntable. On the floor was her wall calendar where "Danny comes!" was written in giant red letters.

I needed to tell her about the phone call. I had to.

"Promise you won't laugh?" she said.

"About what?"

She picked up her drawing pad and turned it my way. It was Dad on a boat, attaching a worm to his hook. Blaire had zoomed in on his face—the squinty eyes, the nose dabbed with sunscreen, the upper lip that jutted out in concentration exactly the way hers did.

"You drew that?"

"It's so weird," she said, gazing into the space between us. "It's like I've been hearing Dad's instructions in my head... Pointers, you know? About drawing? He used to always say that most people drew what they *thought* they saw, not what was actually *there*. And I now I totally get what he..."

Her face blurred and the words faded. *Was* it true? It couldn't have been. Right? Plus, *duh*, Mom would've told us. Some people you'd expect to lie, like James McDonough who in sixth grade told everyone that his house had burned to the ground. Or Nickie Reed who swore that she was once so small that she fit inside a matchbox. Mom wasn't a liar type.

But still I needed to find out for sure. "Sorry, I need to..." and I went toward Mom's room where the whir of her hair dryer sounded like a frantic bee, buzzing through the air.

Flung on her bed was a damp white towel smudged in places from her dark eye makeup. Next to that were two different outfits—two skirts and two blouses, complete with necklaces and scarves, laid flat on the bed the way I used to do in third grade the night before school. On her bedside table was a book titled *Surviving the Death of a Loved One.*

I stood there, trying to figure out what to say when I realized that the green blanket on her bed that had been there forever had now been replaced with a white comforter.

I charged into the bathroom where Mom sat at her vanity, her hair whipping all over the place. She wore the baby chick bathrobe with the missing belt loop.

"Where's the green blanket?" I said.

When she turned around and saw me, she went "Oh!" with her hand on her chest and that surprised look deep in her eyes like what she saw was far worse than just me standing there in the doorway.

"Good Lord, Martie," she said, returning the dryer to her hair. "Can't you ever announce your presence?"

Announce my *presence*? Was she kidding?

"It's Martie Wheeler!" I said in a loud voice. "What happened to the green blanket?"

"I got rid of it."

My heart sank. "You got *rid* of it? Are you serious?"

The dryer blew Mom's hair in all directions, but a strand stuck to her lower lip. "It was all torn up on the bottom," she said. "Plus it was very stained."

Yeah, well, it was probably very stained from my milk spilling out of my bottle when I was a year old. Or from drool that had dripped from the corner of my mouth as I lay there, my little finger rubbing the smooth strip of satin.

Mom turned off the dryer and set it aside. "I can't keep everything, Martie. Life just isn't like that." She reached for her brush and ran it through her hair.

"So what did you do with it?"

"It's in the back of my car. I'll take it to Goodwill on my way to the office. Someone'll want it."

"*I* want it!"

A lump rose in my throat. I bit down on the side of my cheek. *Do not cry over a stupid blanket.* I stepped out of the bathroom and into her bedroom. I made myself focus on her desk where she paid bills, wrote Christmas cards and made doctor and dentist appointments. It was also where I'd snooped and found a series of mushy letters between my parents from when they'd first met.

I turned back to her. She was hunched over the magnifying mirror, lining her eyelids with a brown pencil. Last year she sat me down in front of that same mirror and said, "Those are your pores. It's important to keep them breathing."

"Is there something I'm supposed to know?" I asked her.

"Something like what?" She'd been wearing foundation lately, which hid the dark circles but turned the rest of her face the same tone, like a mannequin's.

"About Dad. Some…"

She squinted at me through the mirror. "Some what?"

I studied her closely, ready for a "Yes, it's true. He killed himself in the basement." I could handle it. I could. I just needed to ask the question. But asking felt like bad luck, as if saying the words might make it true.

"Did he kill himself?" It rushed out of my mouth like vomit.

"What in the world…?" She turned around to me, blinking three times.

"Someone said he did."

"Who?"

"It's not true, is it?" I stared at her mouth, waiting, my nail flicking a loose cuticle.

"What kind of person would tell you something like that?"

"That girl from our house." I wanted to cry. Why couldn't Mom just say yes or no?

"Oh for heaven's sakes. Why would you listen to someone like that?"

My throat swelled. "I don't know." I glanced in the trashcan where an empty container of cover up lay on its side.

"Did you talk to Blaire about this?"

I shook my head no.

"Look at me," she said, locking eyes with mine. She was about to say it. I stared into her dark pupils, which was like staring straight into the sun.

This was it. Oh God, please. Please. Please.

"Your father had a heart attack."

I jumped at the words, swallowed them whole. "Okay."

"That's how he died."

That was it. The final answer.

"Was something wrong with his heart?" My gaze fastened on her mouth, desperate for that last shred of information.

"Not that we knew of," she said. "But obviously…"

I exhaled loudly. I didn't even mean to. "Okay." Something drained out of me. I kept thinking of the words that President Ford had said after he took the oath of office. "Our long national nightmare is over."

Just because Sarah lived in our old house didn't mean that I had to believe what she said. She knew nothing about our family.

"Come here." Mom opened her arms and took me into her robe like she used to do when I was a little girl. I wanted to be that young again, to drift off in her warmth, my mouth open without fearing that a black spider from the basement might crawl inside.

Chapter 9

"I NEED TO find out what's going on with the Hanley girls," I said in the morning as Blaire and I waited for the bus. The weather had shifted overnight and now the air felt sharp against my face.

"They're dead," Blaire said as she picked at the black grip tape that she'd wound around her tennis racquet.

"They're not dead."

"You're so naïve. How could they possibly still be alive? Think about it."

"Oh shut up."

I turned away from her and brought my arms in close around my waist, shivering.

"Autumn's almost here," Dad used to say without consulting a calendar. Or "Snow's just around the corner." When I asked how he always knew, he'd say, "I can feel it in my bones."

I'd never been a cold weather person. The fact book mentioned the lake's "ocean-like swells" in the colder months, which brought to mind "Poseidon Adventure."

I swung around and faced Blaire. "You know that witch?"

"Uh huh." She sounded bored. Or irritated. Maybe yesterday she and Danny had had a fight over the phone.

"She killed her husband and two kids." So *there*.

Not a fraction of worry on her face. Or surprise. She peered down the road for the bus and said, "Uh huh" like it was old—and not very interesting—news.

"Her family all died," I went on.

She glared at me. "You believe everything you hear, don't you?"

"It's a fact. It was in the paper."

The unmistakable squeak of the bus brakes filled the street. Seconds later, it came into view, a goldish-yellow, oversized bug with bulging eyes, barreling toward us.

"It's the truth," I said.

"You need to learn to ask more questions."

"Like what?" I squinted, noticing that her blonde streak had faded.

"Like everything."

———

In English class, Mrs. Neely, who had a pale face and short, spiky hair, told us that we were moving "head first" into "Personal Expressions." Which meant writing about personal experiences and, in particular, one important event in our lives.

"Leave your inhibitions outside this door." She strolled up and down the aisle in her flowy pants and long paisley blouse, handing out composition books to each student. "I want you to be free in this class. Raw."

Raw? What did that mean? Like how I felt when Sarah accused my dad of killing himself in the basement? Like how I felt when I first saw the pictures of the Hanley girls? All I could think about was that phone call. Sarah had sounded so certain. But then Mom had denied it. Fiercely. And now I floated in the middle, not sure whom to believe.

"We'll be taking risks in this class," she said. "Emotional risks."

Why was I the only one in the family with the doubt? Was it, like Blaire had said, because I hadn't accepted that Dad had died? I *had* accepted it, though!

"I want you to go deep," Mrs. Neely said. "Write about everything." After the bell rang, she added, "especially the things that hurt."

———

"Take a Twinkie," Allie said to me at her house. "Take whatever."

We stood in front of their snack cabinet, deciding what to eat. It was the best snack food I'd ever seen. Candy bars, pretzels, chips, Hostess cupcakes. They even had potato chips that were delivered fresh to their house every Tuesday in a big speckled tin.

Allie grabbed a bag of Cheetos and I took the Twinkie and followed her up the stairs to her bedroom, which smelled like scented candles from Spencer Gifts.

"You think those sisters have eaten anything?" she asked, dipping her hand into her bag. I'd told her earlier about the Hanleys but not about what Sarah had told me about my dad. "You think that guy feeds them?"

I tore away the thin plastic wrapping. I couldn't wait to shove all that soft mush in my mouth. "Probably not." The cakey smell drifted up and I breathed it in. My teeth sunk into the moistness, the creamy middle. As my tongue flicked out cream, a sick vision flashed through my mind: the Hanley girls, trapped in a cellar, in their own neighborhood. Or no—not even together. Split up. In darkness. Surrounded by the stink of dead bodies.

Yesterday after school I'd paged through a pile of *Washington Post*s at the local library, devouring and Xeroxing each article about the girls, but I already knew most of the information, like that the sisters were "good girls." They babysat. They always came home on time. And they'd left for the mall that day with only six dollars between them. I couldn't believe they were still missing. *Was* I naïve? Was there a chance they could be alive?

"Look, they're spooning," Allie said, holding up two Cheetos attached to each other. She tossed them in her mouth, licked the orange dust from her fingertips and, from underneath her bed, pulled out a basket full of makeup.

"This makes you really tan." She opened up a small tube and rubbed it into her cheeks. "Want some?"

"Sure."

I smeared the lotion all over my face, hoping it contained an anti-acne component.

"He probably throws them scraps," I said, lining my eyes with a black pencil. "Like they're animals."

She turned to me. "Wait. What?"

"The sisters."

"Oh. Am I tan yet?"

"Not yet. Am I?"

"Nope."

I stroked mascara on my lashes, then ran my pinky finger under my eyes to create a smoky look.

Allie turned up the radio. "I love this song." It was "I Wanna Make it with You" by Bread.

"Is that your dad?" I pointed to a framed photo of a smiling, dark-haired man standing under a sign that read "Lattiker Automobiles."

"Uh huh. That's his dealership." She shoved the basket under the bed. "What about your dad? What does he do?"

"*My* dad?"

"Uh huh."

"Oh. Um. He works—I mean, he used to work in—well, he doesn't anymore, but—"

There was no easy way. First of all, there were the actual words. "He passed" sounded like something a nurse would say. "He passed away" wasn't any better. "He's dead" sounded like he was killed—murdered, even. "He died" was the least horrible, but all prompted a similar reaction: "Oh my *God*. Your *dad*? What happened?"

"He's dead," I finally admitted. "I mean, he died. *And* he's dead." God, I was an idiot.

"*What?*" Allie's eyes narrowed. "*Gahd*, Martie. Was he sick?"

Maybe I just wasn't used to saying it out loud, but my answer always sounded half-finished and, at the same time, weirdly abrupt, like there was something more to the answer. Maybe that was what death was, though—abrupt—and saying it aloud conveyed exactly that.

"D'you not want to talk about it? Cause we don't have to."

"No, it's fine." I sunk in her bed among a jumble of stuffed animals, and she sat at the opposite end. My eyes darted around her room, skimming over the two dark blue bathing suits hanging from her doorknob, the poster of Mark Spitz in the pool, mid-butterfly, coming up for air. I reached for a stuffed monkey and put him on my lap, smoothing my fingers against the soft ears.

"So what happened?" Allie stared at my mouth, waiting. Her skin took on an orange tint. Maybe it was the Cheetos.

"He was at work," I said. "And—"

"How'd you find out? I mean, did they take you out of school and all that?"

I shook my head. "I was at my friend, Robin's." I glanced once more at the poster of Mark Spitz and focused on the droplets of water clinging to his moustache.

"My sister's best friend was killed in a car accident last year," Allie said. "She cried for like the entire year. They made an announcement over the intercom at school. Sharon freaked and left the house for two entire days."

"It was dark when I got home," I told Allie. "The kitchen window was open. Like open with no screens on it."

"How come?"

"I don't know." At the time, I'd thought that maybe a bird had flown in the house and Mom was trying to shoo it out. I remembered the cool air floating in, thinking that it felt like snow.

"Where was Blaire?"

"In the bathroom." Mom had said, "Your sister is out of sorts." I'd never heard her say those words. *Out of sorts.*

"Death isn't supposed to happen until people are old and decrepit," Allie said.

"I know. Plus my dad was healthy. He was—"

A bang on her door made my shoulders jump. "Hey!" A guy's voice.

"Hey what?" Allie yelled back.

The door opened.

He was older, high school, maybe. And standing there like a movie star, eyes all squinty and hair fluffy and clean but not brushed, just shiny the way it gets when you've been at the pool a lot. A slight smile lifted the corners of his mouth as he saw me sitting on the bed. A rush of warmth entered the top of my head, whooshing through my whole body and coming out my fingertips. I felt warm all over.

"You can stop drooling now," Allie said, and for a second I thought she was talking to me.

"I'm Tommy," he said to me, grinning. He wore off-white cords and a faded denim shirt with two pockets in the front.

"I'm Martie."

"She's new," Allie said. "She lives near the witch. And she's got an older sister."

"Her name's Blaire," I said. "Wheeler. She's on the tennis team."

"Long hair? Yeah, I know her."

"Did you ask her out yet?" Allie turned to me. "He's in love with every girl on the planet."

He smiled like it was true and he was proud of it. I kind of admired how comfortable he was with himself. It was like, This is me. Take it or leave it.

"Actually, she's taken," I said. "She's got a boyfriend in college. They're practically married."

"So that's one girl you can scratch off your list," Allie said.

"You're tan," he said to me.

I sat up. "Really?"

"Uh huh." Then he winked at me, and my cheeks got all hot.

After he left, Allie said, "Oh my God, you like him, don't you?"

I shook my head. "No! I don't!"

She sighed like, Yeah sure, Martie.

"No, really. He just... I mean, when he—"

She rolled her eyes. "Girls flip over him. I don't get it."

What I didn't get was, What was there *not* to get?

Chapter 10

"Look! She's got a new one!" Blaire rushed over to my side of the bus.

We were on the way home from school and now the bus stopped smack in front of the witch's yard.

"See that one?" Blaire leaned so close to me that the ends of her hair skimmed my navy corduroys. "The head sticking up over there?"

"They're all heads sticking up." I returned to my composition book where, for the entire ride home, I'd been trying to write down my thoughts. Mrs. Neely had told us to just keep writing until something "authentic" came out of us. Well, so far: nothing, except how people in Wisconsin called water fountains "bubblers" and how they pronounced "car" with a hard r and "pop" like "pap." At home in my desk drawer was a stack of spiral notebooks where I'd written almost every single night for the past four years. Sometimes I recorded entire conversations I'd had that day. Or a funny thing that someone had said.

After Dad died, I closed the book and shoved it in my drawer. Not writing the words "Dad died" convinced me that maybe it didn't even happen. Instead I turned my attention to the dusty "H" book of our World Book Encyclopedia set, reading every single fact I could find about heart attacks, and when I couldn't find an answer, I cracked open Mom's Merck Manual.

"That one's definitely new," Blaire said.

I looked up. It must've been ten feet. A long neck sprouting out of the ground, holding an exaggeratedly long oval face with startled eyes and a circle for a mouth. *The faces represent everyone she's killed.*

Finally, the bus stopped. Up front Shelly Stires stood next to the driver, her arm looped around the pole. She said something to him and laughed, but he didn't laugh. He went "Uh huh" and nodded his head a few times. I bet Tommy liked her. She was cute and popular.

"I wonder if it's stone," Blaire said. "Or maybe it's…"

I just wanted the bus to do its three-point turn and head way to the other end of the street, where we lived. Instead, the door squeaked open and the early October air drifted in.

"Holy shit! There she is!" She grabbed her backpack and pushed me up the aisle. "Go!"

Shelly, now halfway down the stairs, turned to me with her perfect T-zone and said, "Just so you know—Susan doesn't like strangers."

"Who's Susan?" I said.

"The witch. She doesn't like people sitting there, gawking at her house."

Oh *please*. Who'd she think she was—the witch's security guard?

We got off the bus and headed toward the chain link fence.

A chill crawled over my skin. The clouds over the lake were heavy, a bluish color, hanging low. A huge gust of wind whipped my hair in my face, the ends snapping in my eyes.

"Why are we *doing* this?" I said, pushing the mess away from my face.

"Hello?" Blaire called to the woman.

Crouched on the ground, the witch glanced up with a snarled expression like, *Oh what now?* She reminded me of a wild animal pawing at the dirt. Her hair, long and thick, was white as snow. She wore a dark sweatshirt and jeans. Around her neck hung a small blue pouch that swung each time her trowel dug at the earth.

"I love your art work," Blaire said in a soft voice but loud enough so that the woman stopped digging.

"Let's go," I whispered.

"We're not here to bother you," Blaire called out.

"Stop talking to her!" I hissed. "She doesn't want us here."

"We just moved here. Our father died."

The witch looked up, her face softening a tad. Oh, great: She responded to the subject of death. It took her a minute or so to rise from her position on the ground. Dirt covered her knees. Her sweatshirt said, "Miller High Life" and, in smaller letters, "The Champagne of Beers." I'd seen that logo in our fridge. I recalled the distinct "fffft!" when Dad pulled back the tab to open it. Alcohol didn't interest me, but I liked the sound of Dad pouring scotch over ice and Mom pulling out a wine cork.

The witch took a step in our direction and I felt like I was about to be swallowed up. She focused on Blaire, though, who gazed back at her like she was a prophet.

Up close she was wrinkly. With piercing light blue eyes. Mom would say, "I bet in her day she was quite a beauty."

She was only five feet away. Thank God the fence divided us.

"And what do you like here?" she said to both of us, and I thought, *Nothing. I like nothing here.*

Blaire studied the strangely littered yard, her eyes going from one bizarre face to another. She tucked her hair behind her ears, a nervous habit from when she was younger. Nervous was definitely not how I'd describe her now. Sad, angry—yes, but not nervous. Finally she pointed at a skeletal figure made out of sticks. "That one looks like a real person, but then it's…" She scrunched up her nose, trying to find the right word.

"I like to absorb everything I come in contact with," the witch said. She had crow's feet like my dad's. She felt for the worn blue pouch around her neck, as if making sure it was still there, then pressed it against her chest. "I believe we can express ourselves through a piece of driftwood. A stone."

Blaire nodded slowly like finally she found someone who spoke her language.

The woman put a tiny silver key into a padlock and I heard the click as it unlocked. "Come take a look if you like." The gate swung open.

The wind shook the leaves out of the trees. A shot of adrenaline rushed through my veins. The Hanley sisters could've said no to that man, but they didn't. They went with him. And now the witch asked us to come with her.

"Sure!" Blaire said.

I cleared my throat. "Ahm, Blaire?"

She swung around and stared so deeply into my eyes that I felt the sting of disgust. I was a pathetic scared little sister, nothing in the world was as clear at that moment.

"Remember what I told you?" I bulged my eyes. Another gust of wind swayed the branches, making mobiles swing in the eeriest way.

"Go home," she said like I was a lost dog.

"Coming?" the witch said, sizing us up, trying to figure out which one to kill first.

"I have homework," I said in my most polite voice. "Thank you, though."

I turned to Blaire, but she was already inside the witch's world, the gate closing firmly behind her.

⇒⊢⊩⇐

At home I went straight to the freezer and took out the bucket of fudge swirl ice cream. It was the only non-healthy food in our house.

I grabbed the Wisconsin fact book and stood at the counter, leafing through the pages while eating around the edges of the ice cream container, where it got melty first. If Dad were alive, he'd grab a spoon and say, "Move over. Let me get in there." Then he'd bring out the Hershey's syrup and drizzle it on top like the final touch on a sand castle.

State bird: Robin

State animal: Badger

State wildlife animal: White tailed deer

State domestic animal: Dairy cow

State fish: Muskellunge

State beverage: Milk

I pushed the book aside. Maybe that gross man with the moustache didn't take the Hanley girls. Maybe it was a woman. She could've stopped them on their way home, rolled down her car window and said, "Can you help me find my puppy?" All a person needed was to get them in a car. From there, they could drive them wherever they wanted. Countless times

I'd pictured myself as one of the girls, stepping into the stranger's car, thinking he was about to offer ice cream or a ride home, and then the horrible moment when he turned onto the highway and the sinking realization that he wasn't driving anywhere near home.

The roof of my mouth was numb. I put away the ice cream and headed toward the stairs. On the foyer table was the newspaper. *White House Tapes Reveal Nixon's Cover-up: Former President Repeatedly Tried to Conceal His Involvement in Watergate Affair.*

As I climbed the stairs to the second floor, I wondered what Dad would've thought about the President of the United States lying to the country. Repeatedly. Maybe he would've defended him the same way Mom had been doing.

"*Damn*it!"

I rushed to Mom's bedroom. Usually she didn't come home until five, but today she was on her hands and knees, scrubbing a spot in the carpet.

"It fell *right* from my grasp." She dipped the washcloth into the pot of sudsy water, squeezed, and pressed it to the carpet.

"Why are you home?" Her wearing a bathrobe in the middle of the day was weird enough; she'd never been the type to lounge around. Plus why wasn't she at work? I glanced around her room for an answer. "Are you sick?" The bedside table held aspirin, a magazine and a half-drunk glass of water. A bottle of red nail polish—the culprit—sat on top of her desk.

"I just can't get this *damn*..." She scrubbed more and a thick lather appeared, oozing deep in the roots of the rug.

"Mom?"

Finally she looked up at me, squinting, like maybe her eyes needed to adjust. Was she drunk? Maybe the water was actually vodka. She tossed the rag and repositioned herself so that her legs jutted straight in front of her like a doll made to sit for a tea party. Her robe parted, exposing a triangular patch of thigh.

"Did something happen?" As usual, my mind raced to catastrophes.

Mom's fingers pressed against her temples. "I told him I'd pick up Chinese food on my way home from the conference." Her hair was greasy, the way mine gets when I've been sick for a few days. "I *hated* those real estate conferences! I can't understand *why* I even went. If I hadn't gone, I would've been home sooner and then I bet he…"

The wind rattled the windows and the room darkened. I waited for a crack of thunder or a flash of lightning, but nothing happened. Just a slow dimming.

"I shouldn't've gone," she said in a small voice.

"Mom." I crouched down next to her, my knees cracking. "He had a heart attack. It wasn't like you could've prevented it."

"But maybe if I'd…" Her breath smelled metallic and it reminded me of the day of the funeral, before people had arrived, when she coached us on what to say to people. "Thank them for coming," she said, her eyelid twitching from not enough sleep. "Tell them they meant a lot to your father."

Now her chin dropped to her chest, and her shoulders began to shake. No sound except a soft ticking from the back of her throat.

I reached for her hand. My mood ring brushed against her wedding band, making a soft but solid clink, which I took as a sign that, even though my lame effort at affection bordered on pathetic, we were deeply connected.

"You'll be okay," I said.

She nodded quickly like, *I know, I know.*

The sky cracked and finally the rain poured down, sheets of it.

Mom's hand let go of mine and reached for the toilet paper roll. She blew her nose. She tore off more squares and blew again. Over and over. It kept coming. She sat there, nodding to herself like, *I can do this.* And she could. She could pour out a certain amount, then screw on the top when it started to overflow.

She stood, wiping her hands on the side of her robe. "Carol Specter says the heavy feeling never goes away."

I too stood. "Mrs. Specter from Maryland?"

She disappeared into the bathroom. "Uh huh."

Mrs. Specter lived at the end of the block and was the owner of Arlo, that dog who prowled inside his wooden fence and barked at everyone. After Dad died, Mrs. Specter brought us casseroles, which was nice but weird considering that we barely knew her.

"She lost her husband a few years back," Mom said, now in a skirt and blouse. Had she even gone to work? "She says it never goes away. It just gets a little bit easier."

The front door opened and I could hear Blaire stomping her feet like she was trying to loosen snow from the bottom of her boots, but there was no snow. Just rain.

"Mom?"

"Hm?"

"That morning did he talk about his chest feeling tight or any of that?"

She stood at the mirror, dabbing cover-up under her eyes. "Haven't we been over this?"

"Had he been nauseous? Because that's one of the symptoms."

A brush of rouge on each cheek. She backed up to view herself. "I'm showing that house at four-thirty."

I ignored her plans. "So when you got home from the conference, did someone from Dad's office call? Or…?"

I tried to picture Mom with the phone pressed to her ear, her eyes narrowing as she struggled to piece the words together. What exactly did they tell her? "He had a heart attack and died"? Or just "He died"?

"Wait," I said, backing up. "Who called and told you what happened? His boss?"

Mom stared at me like I'd crossed an invisible line. Like I was supposed to know exactly what I could and couldn't ask.

⊸┼┼⊷

"I *love* her."

Blaire, in just her white bra and underwear, sat on her light blue carpet, leafing through a large hardback book of paintings. She must've gotten caught in the rain—her wet jeans, shirt and sweatshirt were strewn on the carpet like she'd peeled them off in a rush and flung them in every direction.

"Who?" I asked even though I knew exactly who. I just didn't want to hear about Blaire's growing fascination with her.

"She's a real person. A real artist."

I stood before her mirror. My face was green from the grainy acne mask I'd smeared on my face minutes earlier.

"She listens, you know?" Blaire went on. "She really thinks about what you're saying."

"Yeah, the Hanley sisters probably thought the exact same thing when their kidnapper was talking to them and figuring out how to shove them in his car."

"Every inch of her house is art," she gushed, totally ignoring my comment. "Drawings, sculptures, ceramics. And on all the windowsills she's got these clay figurines that she made when she was my age. Oh my God. It's *so* cool."

I faced her. "I can't believe you went inside her house."

I expected a glare and a "You're so paranoid" but she just stopped on a page and took in a painting of a rust-colored building that was half in sun and half in shade.

"Her husband and sons were *killed*," I reminded her. "It's a fact."

She looked up. Clumps of hair loosened from her braid gave her a wild look that I suddenly envied. "You know what she said?"

I could hardly wait to hear.

"'The body never forgets.'" She recited the words as if she were on stage, quoting Shakespeare.

"What's that supposed to mean?" I rolled the grainy mask residue between my thumb and forefinger and flicked it.

"Stuff that happened to you? Like bad stuff? It's all there, inside you. She said my stuff is gonna come out in my art work."

"What about my stuff?" I pictured a moss-colored liquid shooting out of my pores.

"I don't know." She turned the page. "I guess it'll come out at some point."

"Like in my forehead?"

She shrugged. "Who knows? Maybe in your writing."

Well, that wasn't happening. Nothing was coming out in my writing except lame Wisconsin facts.

Chapter 11

"THE HOLIDAYS ARE coming up," Mom said as she flipped through a sale rack at Gimbel's Department Store. She wore a new red lipstick and blush that she'd applied in the car on the way over. Her camel's hair coat sat on her shoulders. As a young girl, I'd held her gloved hand as she rushed through department stores, the soft coat flapping against my little face.

"Danny'll be here for Thanksgiving," she went on. "I was thinking maybe we could have Julie over, too." She inspected a long, itchy-looking brown sweater, checked the price tag, then tossed it over her arm. "And maybe my boss, Jack."

Ugh. The holidays. I pictured us at the dining room table with Dad's empty chair and a big turkey in the center. Who would carve it? Who would make it? Dad was the cook in the family, not Mom.

"Maybe we could just ignore the holidays this year," I said, going towards a pile of sweaters and dragging my fingertips against the softness. I picked up a light blue and yellow Fair Aisle sweater, the kind a lot of girls in Wisconsin wore, and checked the price. Way too expensive. But I needed clothes, sweaters in particular. Winter was supposed to be horrible in Wisconsin. Tons of snow. Feet and feet of it. I wasn't prepared for that kind of cold.

"Well," Mom said, moving to the next rack, wearing her shopper's face *Yes No No No Yes*. "I'm hoping that when Thanksgiving comes along, we'll all be a little more in the mood."

"In the mood for what? Celebrating?" I checked another tag on a different-ent colored sweater. Still too expensive.

"Well, not exactly, but maybe we'll—"

"*I* won't." I couldn't imagine celebrating anything. The Hanley parents definitely wouldn't celebrate. No stockings on the fireplace. Most likely, no tree. I wondered if Mr. Hanley remembered anything about the last day he'd seen his girls. And what about the mom? She lived far away. In one of the articles, the dad talked about how when the girls returned, he'd let them get their ears pierced. Like they were on a trip with a definite return date.

"We need to be open to new ways of doing things," Mom said, reading the label on the back of a skirt. "We can't be stuck in our old ways."

"Why? What's wrong with tradition?"

"Nothing. But we should be open, that's all."

I hated the way she talked: *We need to, We can't be, We should.* Like a deadline loomed overhead. I wondered if she was still pretending that Dad was on a long trip.

"Why *was* he cremated, anyway?" I asked, moving to the dress rack across from her.

"'Why'?" A line indented her forehead. "Because it was what he wanted."

I blinked. "To be cremated? He told you that?" I flipped through a few dresses.

"Uh huh."

"It just comes up in normal conversation?"

"Mmhm." But it was a faraway "Mmhm," the one she used to placate me, like when I was eight, doing handstands and calling "Mom! Look!"

A dress with fake diamonds dotting the neckline caught my attention and when I reached out to touch one of the jewels, it fell onto the floor.

"Did you see him after he died?"

A slight pause, then a hardness in her light green eyes. "Yes, Martie." An edge had creeped into her voice.

I didn't care. He was my father and I had a right to know what happened. Blaire was right: I needed to ask more questions. "Did he look like... I mean, did he seem like he was..."

"He looked like he was sleeping."

"Really? Sleeping?" It was the kind of thing you'd say to a small child. *He was sleeping before he drifted up to Heaven.*

Besides Dad, the only people I'd known who'd died were my grandparents, but we'd expected that. They were old. And Mom seemed weirdly relieved about Grandma dying, I guess because of their bad relationship. Dad, though—his death came out of the blue.

Or maybe it didn't. Maybe Mom knew something that we didn't. Maybe when he went to the hospital for that virus, the doctor told Mom that it was only a matter of time before he'd have a heart attack.

"When your heart stops," I asked, "do your eyes close or ... I guess they stay open, right?"

Her cold glare cut to my core. "Why would you be interested in such morbid details? It's dis*tur*bing, Martie. What's wrong with you?" She shot me a final glance before turning away and heading for the perfume and makeup section, where a woman wearing a white lab coat and pink lipstick stood, holding a bottle and saying, "A spray? A spray? Would you like a spray?"

"Please," Mom said, yanking up her coat sleeve, as if a new fragrance might mask the questions that still lingered between us.

Chapter 12

"This is your life line," Allie told me, dragging her index finger against my palm. It was two days before Thanksgiving, and we were in sleeping bags on my carpet because my bed was too small for both of us.

"This line indicates a noble quality," she said, chewing a wad of Bazooka.

"*Noble*?" I said. "How boring can you get? What about love lines?"

"Okay." She bent back my fingers to get a better view of the lines, then tapped right in the center of my palm, which tickled. "Right there. That's the marriage line. It says…you'll be marrying…Ahhhhmmmm, let's see…. Tommy! And having three babies with him!"

"Hilarious." Whenever I pictured myself with a boyfriend, all I envisioned was me worrying that popcorn was stuck between my teeth or that my broken out forehead blinked like a neon sign. If he leaned in to kiss me, I'd probably jerk back and blurt out some stupid Wisconsin fact like, "Did you know that Sheboygan is the bratwurst capital of the world?"

Allie reached in her backpack and rubbed Carmex on her lips.

"Wait," I said. "Can you look again?" I held out my hand. "Can you see anything in there about my dad?" With my other hand, I grabbed a piece of Bazooka, tore off the wrapping without reading the comic and stuffed it in my mouth.

"Like what?" She squinted like she was peering into a microscope.

"Anything. Just look, okay?" I chomped down on the gum and the sugar granules dissolved in my teeth.

Mom and Dad both pursed their lips tightly when they concentrated. Allie did the opposite. Her mouth hung open as she moved her fingertip over my palm, trying to find answers from the lines in my hand.

Downstairs, the vacuum cleaner rattled like it sucked up something it shouldn't have.

"What does it say?" I stared at her shiny lips.

"There's not like, a 'Dad' line." She let go of my hand. "Don't worry, though. You're noble. Plus you'll live a long life with my brother."

"Very funny." I shimmied into my sleeping bag and lay there, staring up at the ceiling light fixture, wondering if it was screwed in tight enough.

"Tommy's a total flirt, so don't expect anything," she said.

"I won't," I lied.

If a person decided to kill himself, he also decided to leave his family. To leave everyone and everything. And that definitely wasn't Dad. He loved us. That I knew. Not in a million years would he leave us like that.

After I turned out the light, Allie said, "You think those girls are actually alive?"

"A lot of people are working on the case," I said, as if I had inside information.

More rattling from the vacuum. Like a spoon caught in a blender. Mom turned it off and I heard her bang it against the stair, trying to loosen whatever object was caught inside.

I doubled my pillow and faced her. "What would you do if someone told you that someone in your family killed themselves?"

"*What?*" The moon was weirdly bright and, even in the dark, I could see her face perfectly—the eyes that were close together, the turned up nose that she hated, the full lips that I wished I had. "Why are you asking this?"

"That girl who I talk to in Maryland?"

"Yeah?"

"She said my dad did that in our cellar."

Her sleeping bag rustled. "Wait. I'm confused. I thought you said he had a heart attack."

"He did! She's trying to freak me out."

"But he's your *dad*. Why would *she* know anything?"

Good question. Had I not felt that pinch of doubt, I wouldn't have given the words another thought, but little by little they'd seeped into me, like how that red polish had sunk into Mom's carpet.

"Maybe someone actually did do that in your old house," Allie said, yawning. "Like fifty years ago or something."

I nodded. "Maybe." That was true. I hadn't thought of that.

"But *sui*cide," she said. "*Gahd.* Can you imagine?"

"No." I got up and flicked on the black and white T.V. that I'd borrowed from Mom for the night. "Love, American Style" was just beginning.

"Leave this!" Allie said.

I got back in my sleeping bag. Davy Jones was in the first episode. The laugh track came on after the characters spoke, but I didn't think any of it was funny. I looked over at Allie and she was squinting like she was trying to get it. Blaire would say that we were too young to understand the humor. I hated when she said stuff like that. She acted like I couldn't handle anything. I was almost fourteen.

By the time the episode was over, Allie was asleep. I turned off the T.V. and pulled the green blanket off my bed and brought it close to me, breathing in all those years when I was too young to ever think that my mom might not be telling me the truth.

Allie looked completely different with her eyes closed. Mom said that when Dad was dead, he looked like he was sleeping. Allie didn't look dead. Not even close.

After drifting off, I woke, starved, at 2:30 in the morning with a gnawing hunger that felt like someone had reached into my stomach and scooped out any last remnant of food.

I went down to the kitchen. It was weird to be the only one up in all that darkness and quiet. I opened the fridge and the light pooled around my feet. The shelves held the same items that Mom bought every time she went to the grocery store: cheese, milk, wheat germ, ground beef, iceberg lettuce. I missed Dad's purchases—English muffins, smoked fish, lemons, grape juice.

I took out the loaf of Roman Meal bread and the peanut butter and made a sandwich. Peanut butter and jelly without the jelly. I poured a glass of milk, ate half the sandwich and was headed back upstairs when I glanced in the living room. Mom, in yesterday's work clothes, was spread on the couch, her legs tucked up around her chest, her lips puckered like a child's. On the floor was the book that must've fallen from her hands—*On Death and Dying: The Five Stages of Grief.* There were *stages* of grief? I wondered if doubt was one of them.

Upstairs I went into her room, set my half sandwich and milk on top of the desk, and grabbed a light blue wool blanket from her closet. I carried it downstairs and spread it over her.

Nope. She didn't look dead, either.

I went back to her room and sat on the edge of her bed, picking apart pieces of the sandwich and methodically depositing them in my mouth. The only remnant of Dad was the photo on the dresser of him and Mom, but Dad wore sunglasses and you could barely make out who he was. I wanted to see his ties and suits and a striped pajama leg sticking out of the hamper.

Mom's desk had three big drawers for papers and then five small ones on top for things like stamps, tacks, paper clips, the occasional coin or rubber band. As a young girl, I'd pull open the drawers again and again, each time hoping that something new would appear.

The thing was, I trusted Mom. I did. Why *wouldn't* I? She swore he'd had a heart attack, and I believed her. But ever since that phone call, a lens had clicked into focus—not perfect focus; it was like borrowing someone else's glasses that made you see just a tiny bit better than your own.

I drank the rest of my milk. Cold trickled down to my stomach. I set the glass on the desk and pulled open a drawer that was crammed with home-made cards from us, Blaire's letters from camp, birthday cards in my bubbly handwriting back when I dotted my i's with hearts. A brown envelope that said "Report Cards" in Mom's urgent capital letters.

The third drawer produced a huge bright blue folder bulging with papers. I took it out and felt the weight of it. Old bills. Bank statements. A Ford packet about the Mustang. Insurance stuff. Why would she even keep that stuff?

A red folder with the word "Medical" written on it caught my eye. Health records. I pulled out a bunch of bills. I moved over to the window where the moonlight streamed in. A Washington Hospital Center bill. That was where Dad stayed when he had that virus. I flipped through more paper. A business card fell out. *Dr. Harold Winston, Psychiatrist.*

Whoa. For Dad? Maybe he actually had gone. I liked that we shared the desire to sit in a quiet place and have someone hear what we had to say. Then again, maybe he never even went. That too we'd have in common.

I was about to return the folder to the drawer when Mom, in a way-too-awake voice, said, "What are you doing in here?"

I jumped a mile. I hadn't even heard her come up the stairs.

Her work skirt and shirt were rumpled; her mascara had smudged under her eyes. And a deep groove had settled across her cheek where the seam of the couch must've been.

"I was just..." I gestured to the desk with my hand that wasn't holding the psychiatrist's number. "...looking for an envelope." My heart pounded under my nightgown. The red numbers of her digital clock said 2:59. I couldn't remember ever being awake with her at that hour.

She glanced at my guilty hand that held the business card. "Well, I don't like you sneaking around like this." Her eyes darted around the room, suspicious. "Did you bring *food* in here?"

"No," I lied. "Just milk."

"Well I don't want *milk* or any other drink in this room. What's the matter with you?"

I started to sink into a hole but made myself snap out of it by closing the desk drawers that I'd left open and heading out of the room. My foot stepped right on the nail polish stain. It was actually more noticeable now than before, like all of Mom's scrubbing had done just the opposite of what she'd wanted.

Chapter 13

BLAIRE SHRIEKED WHEN she saw Danny at the airport. She threw her arms around him and he picked her up and twirled her. It was like a scene out of "Love Story" before Ali MacGraw got sick. After they finished kissing, they hugged for a long time, which, to me, meant a lot more than just "This is my boyfriend." Blaire's whole body spoke. *This is what I'm getting*, it said. *Love*. A heaviness tugged at me, the way I felt when I peered through a tiny sliver and saw the undeniable truth that Dad was never coming back. Ever.

In the backseat, they sat with their thighs pressed against each other's, their fingers interlaced.

I fiddled with the radio dial, which was freezing against my fingertips. "Midnight at the Oasis" played.

Mom turned down the volume and, peering in the rear view mirror, asked, "How's everything in Maryland?"

"Great," Danny said.

Mom hummed to herself. She'd been in a good mood ever since she sold two houses in one week.

The air smelled like baking bread, which meant that we were passing one of the three breweries—Miller, Pabst or Schlitz.

"Day after tomorrow we'll have a nice Thanksgiving dinner," Mom said, squinting into the setting sun.

But Thanksgiving was Dad's thing. He'd buy the turkey and pull out the slimy giblets and set them aside for gravy. I'd help him balance the bird in the sink so that the water could run through the cavity and then be wiped out with a paper towel and patted dry like a baby after a bath.

"So how you doin', Marts?" Danny leaned forward and sort of squeezed my arm. My skin tingled. If only he knew how many times I'd stood in front of Dannyland, imagining I was kissing him—or anyone, really. Blaire got to do that all the time. I wanted to know how it felt to really love someone the way she did and to be loved back.

"How's our house in Maryland?" I asked, turning in my seat so I could have a good view of him. "Have you seen the people who live there?"

"Nope." His dimple was crazy. It lit up his whole face. Or maybe it was the eyes that gleamed when he smiled. Or the teeth.

"What about the Hanley girls?" I asked. He must've known the latest news. "What's going on with them?" I figured every kid and parent in Maryland were as obsessed with the case as I was.

"Who?"

"The sisters," I said. "You know."

"No, he doesn't know," Blaire said like Danny couldn't speak for himself. "And he doesn't care."

"I care," Danny said, smiling that smile and winking at me.

But then he grabbed Blaire and kissed her right smack on the lips and I turned back around, cheeks hot with envy.

———

I sat in my room with all the Hanley articles spread out over my yellow carpet like they were pieces of a puzzle that I was trying to solve. I kept looking at the sketch of the moustached guy who'd been hanging around the mall the day they disappeared. No way did those girls get in a car with that creep.

In my closet, I found a loose-leaf fake denim binder from last year. I'd written all over the front with a blue ballpoint pen, stuff like "Robert Redford" and "Peter Frampton" in bubble letters. Dad was still alive when I wrote those things. Now everything had changed. Even my cursive looked different then—lighter, loopier. I rubbed my finger against the handwriting as if, with one touch, I could be transported back to that time before grief, suspicion and worry took over my thoughts.

I replaced the binder with fresh paper and got to work.

The very first article was from April 30. I'd been so focused on the content of the articles that I hadn't really noticed the dates, but somehow reading *April 30, 1974* on the top of the page made me feel sick all over again. Patty Hearst had been kidnapped, too, but we also saw her on the news. Everyone knew she was still alive. Brainwashed, but alive. Every time I thought, *Maybe I do need to face the facts*, another part of me said, *No*. But as I taped each article to a new page, my *No* voice was no louder than a whisper.

———

In the morning the car movers arrived with the Mustang.

I rushed down the stairs like a kid on Christmas morning, grabbed my coat and stood outside in the bitter cold until the wheels touched the freezing pavement. Candied apple red. Black interior. White hood. The hubcaps, which I used to polish with Turtle Wax until they sparkled, were covered in grime.

I heard Mom's heels scurry across the paved driveway. Her perfume trailed behind her like a long, sheer scarf.

One of the guys from the moving van handed her a clipboard. She signed something and he ripped off a pink sheet of paper, said, "Thank you, ma'am," and returned to his van while she disappeared inside the house without barely a glance at the car, which was exactly what she did the first time Dad came home with it.

"Impulsive," she'd called him, turning away with that disgusted sneer. When he quit his job in January, she called him that, also. And "'irresponsible."

"We have a *family*," Mom reminded him. Like he'd forgotten that. "You can't just quit your job."

The car had been a great purchase. The boat, on the other hand, bordered on crazy. Part of me loved that Dad just went for it. A classic "Live for the moment" purchase. But Mom had been right—"impulsive." Next to Mom yelling at Grandma, it was the maddest I'd ever seen her.

I opened the heavy passenger door and crouched down to get into the back seat, where I always sat. The distinct smell of leather and gasoline hit me in the gut and for a second I couldn't find my breath. Blaire, Dad and I spent hours in the car with the top down, pulling over at yard sales, swinging by Magruder's Grocery for dinner items. We'd drive up to Gifford's where we sat outside, the summer sun softening our mint chip cones. What was wrong with impulsive? Impulsive was fun.

I tipped back my head and let it rest against the back of my seat, then I drew in a deep breath and blew it out like I was exhaling smoke. My eyes scanned the dusty black dashboard and the glove compartment where Dad kept cigarettes.

Keys! They were in the ignition. Dad's silver keys with the tiny Mustang imprinted on it. I crawled up front and planted myself in the driver's seat. The black steering wheel was cold against my hands. I pushed in the silver cigarette lighter and watched it pop up. I just sat there, trying to imagine myself as Dad, peering through the rear view mirror, calling back to us, "How 'bout an ice cream?"

I turned the ignition one notch, then flipped on the radio, which only came on when I hit my fist against the dashboard. There. Casey Kasem. The countdown. I caught the very end of "When Will I See You Again?"

I wished I could remember the last thing I'd said to Dad. Probably something stupid. What I could recall was the dinner he'd made the night before he died—grilled chicken wings with lemon wedges on top, and cornbread. Our favorite.

Mom kept licking her fingers, saying, "Boy that tastes good!" and "I don't know *why* I'm so hungry!" We polished off everything except five wings and two pieces of cornbread, which I wrapped in tin foil and stuck in the fridge, already planning the next day's meal. But we didn't eat much after he died. Cereal, mostly. Whenever I opened the fridge, the slightest glimpse of the silver foil made me feel sick. Still though, I wanted to devour that chicken, not because I was hungry, but because I didn't want to abandon the last thing he'd cooked for us. It ended up stinking up the fridge until someone—Mom, probably—tossed it in the trash.

"Kung Fu Fighting" came on next. I sang to the very end and, even though my fingertips had turned white and my butt was nearly frozen to the seat, I stayed through the next song, breathing in the last bit of summer before returning to the numbing cold.

Chapter 14

"So is your boss still coming for Thanksgiving?" I asked Mom about an hour later as I sat at the kitchen table, eating cold eggs, which were slimy against my tongue. My new binder sat on the table next to my plate.

"Mmhm." She wore her open house clothes—heels and hose, a brown skirt, her favorite peach sweater and her long gold snaky necklace with the round locket at the end. "You'll like him," she said, wiping the frying pan dry and shoving it in the bottom cabinet. "He's very attentive."

I broke a piece of bacon in half and it snapped. "What does that mean? Do you like him or something?" The idea of Mom dating hadn't even occurred to me, but of course it was a possibility. A huge possibility. Mom was pretty and single although I preferred to see her as a widow in black who'd never remarry. I couldn't believe how stupid I'd been. Jack Moyer. Of *course*. Maybe he was the whole reason we'd moved in the first place.

"Oh, no no no," Mom said, smiling in a coy way while she stuck the last of Danny and Blaire's breakfast plates in the dishwasher. "He's just a nice man, that's all." She kneeled to sponge a spot on the floor, which made her locket swing like a pendulum.

"Is he married?"

"No," she said, rising. "He lives alone."

She could've said *He's not married*, which would've been a normal answer, but *He lives alone* sounded like she'd been to his apartment and seen his bedroom.

"He's a bachelor," she explained.

Oh great. A bachelor. I pictured Mom as a contestant on "The Dating Game" saying, "Bachelor Number One..." and asking him some embarrassing question like, "What's your idea of a romantic evening?"

"Maybe he and Julie'll hit it off," I said, hoping she'd whisk him away from Mom, but I couldn't imagine Julie hitting it off with anyone except a guy who had a bunch of problems and didn't mind being squeezed to death when she hugged him.

"Julie doesn't seem to be too interested in dating," Mom said, going to her purse and rummaging inside.

"What about you?" I said, wishing I never brought up the subject of Jack Moyer. But I couldn't stop myself. "Are you ... interested in that?"

Thank God Mom said, "No, I'm really not," but she was probably just saying that so I wouldn't freak out. Either way, I didn't push it.

I opened my binder and flipped through the pages, stopping on an article I hadn't fully read. *Abduction Specialists Reveal Possible Scenarios.*

"Blaire's coach called yesterday," Mom said. "Apparently she hasn't been going to her practices."

Most abductions are carried out by family members or someone the child knows and trusts. It made me sick, thinking that they might've jumped into an uncle's car, assuming he'd drive them home.

"Do you know anything about that?" Mom said.

I looked up. She pulled off the cap of a red felt tip pen and wrote something on a yellow pad.

"What?" I said. "No."

One specialist said that the kidnapper could've grabbed the sister in the mall parking lot and threatened to hurt her if the other one didn't comply. Another one made my heart sink: A man told the girls that he was on his way to the pet store to buy his daughter a puppy or kitten and which one did the girls think he should get? An hour or so later, when the girls were walking home, the man would pull up to them and call out the window, "I got the puppy! Let me show you!"

"Martie, this is important," Mom said.

I looked up again. Her grey roots were starting to show.

"I'm worried about her," she went on.

"Well I have heart palpitations and no one seems to worry about *that*."

"You're stable," she threw back at me as she shoved the pad and pen back in her purse. "I'm not worried about you."

"Blaire's not stable?"

"It's not that," she said, her fingertips reaching toward a crack in the wall. "It's her reactions to things. That's what worries me." The crack climbed about two feet, then dipped sharply as if drawn by an unsteady hand.

"I don't like seeing this," she said, moving her finger along it the same way Allie traced the lines of my hand, trying to see my future.

I hated how she jumped from worry to worry. From Blaire not going to tennis practice to Blaire's reactions to the crumbling house. I turned the page with a little too much force and the bottom of the paper ripped.

"These cracks are everywhere!" She inspected a longer one that rose up from behind the stove. "When did this happen?"

Like I knew. It was the way she got with Dad, especially towards the end. *What would make you do something as stupid as quitting your job? How can you not under*stand *this?* Thinking about that infuriated me now. Who cared if he quit his job? He wanted to paint! Mom acted like we'd end up living on the street. But that wasn't the case. She had money, and plenty of it. She just didn't want him to know about it.

"What's that?" she said, standing over me now.

I picked up my plate and headed for the sink. "Just some stuff about the kidnapping," I said under my breath.

"Oh *Martie*, for God's *sake!*" She turned away, disgusted. "Why in the world would you still be focused on that?"

What was *her* problem? Talk about reactions! "Why does it matter? It's *my* binder." I flipped on the water and watched the eggs slide off the plate.

"I don't think reading about this case helps you."

I turned around, water dripping from my fingertips. "Helps me with what?"

"How long has it been? April? May?"

I shut off the water. "They're alive."

"The chances are highly—"

"They're two girls!" I yelled, rushing to the binder and slamming it closed. "They could've been me and Blaire! How can you not care about them?"

"Honey," Mom said, coming toward me, which only made me back away. "Of course I *care*, but there's a point when you have to tell yourself that…"

"That what?" I said. "That they're on a long trip?"

She ignored me and left the room. *Clickclickclick* Her heels stopped at the hall closet door.

"Did Dad know that you inherited that money?" I called to her from the kitchen. I wanted to trap her.

"I don't like your tone," she said when I reached the hallway.

"Before we moved," I said, wanting to scream it but telling myself to be calm, "you said we could afford this house because of the money you inherited."

"Yes, that's true." Mom took out her camel's hair coat and her arms disappeared in the sleeves. A quick fluff of the hair.

"So….?" I said, waiting for her to continue.

"I know what you're getting at. You think I hid money from your father. And you know what? I did." She shut the closet door and pulled on brown leather gloves that she'd bought for three dollars at Heavenly Threads, a church thrift store.

"So he *didn't* know that you inherited it."

"Your father loved you girls," she said. "But he wasn't thinking about anyone's future."

"Because he was into the 'here and now,'" I said with a dwindling touch of pride in my voice. "That's why."

"Mm," she murmured like the "Here and Now" wasn't such a great thing to be into. She reached for her purse and flung it over her shoulder, spritzing the air with the perfume bottle she kept on the hat shelf of the closet.

"Why are you so mad at him?" I said.

"Your *father*? I'm not mad at him." Her hand grabbed at the keys, which sat on the mail table in the foyer.

"You never even went for a ride in the Mustang! Why did you have to punish him? He got the car for *all* of us!"

She squinted at me like I was a tiny bug she wanted to squash with the heel of her hand. "Don't you *dare* start acting like that sister of yours." She pointed her finger at me. "That's the *last* thing I need!"

She tightened her coat belt and left in a haze of perfume that was so strong it made the back of my throat hurt.

⚔

"Did you go to the witch's?" I asked Danny when he and Blaire came back from their walk.

He leaned against the counter, his perfect teeth plunging into a green apple; Blaire stood at the opened fridge, staring into the cold like she was looking at something more vast and complicated than refrigerated food on shelves. *That sister of yours.* Like Blaire was evil. All I'd done was ask Mom why she'd been so mad at Dad. But now I got the distinct feeling that if I wanted the answers about what happened the day Dad died, I needed to find them myself. Fine. I could do that.

"We saw someone flying in the air," Danny said. "I think on a broomstick?"

"She buried her family in her yard," I told him, taking out the cereal and a bowl.

"Martie, shut up," Blaire said.

"Did you actually see her?" I reached over Blaire and grabbed the milk.

"Oh yeah, we saw her all right," he said, tossing his apple core in the trash. "First she rose up from the ground and then she took off on her broom and flew way over the lake."

I laughed. I loved him.

"It's not funny," Blaire said. "She's a real person. How would you like it if you were known as the witch?"

With the back of my spoon, I pushed the Corn Chex under the milk. Mom preferred Grape Nuts, which sounded like gravel sloshing around in her mouth.

"People here eat cheese curds," I told Danny, switching into fact mode. "Isn't that weird? They actually have contests where people have to eat like half a pound."

Danny laughed. "That's disgusting."

"I know, but it's a real thing." I spooned up a pile of cereal and shoved it in my mouth. "At cheese festivals." But the load of cereal in my mouth made it sound like "Keys fessvil."

Blaire slammed the fridge door. "There's no food in this house."

I swallowed and, in Mom's voice, said, "Make an egg drink."

"Have some cheese curds," Danny said, slinking in back of Blaire and wrapping his arms around her.

"Let's go to the store," she said, trying to wriggle out of his grasp.

"You can't drive the Mustang," I said. "It needs the right tags or something."

"Danny!" she screamed as he tickled her. A tickle that turned into a mini make-out session.

"Guys! Please!" I said like they were deeply offending me, but in truth I was taking mental notes for that one day when Tommy and I would make out in the backseat of his blue Pacer.

"Don't be such a prude," Blaire said. They untangled themselves and went toward the door, their ski jackets swishing with each step.

I sat there for a second before bolting out of my seat and grabbing my coat.

Out front Blaire had backed the Mustang out of the garage. It hummed. It was the sound of Dad. The sound of him saying, "Who wants to go for a ride?" The sound of something fun about to happen.

Before I could say, "Wait! I'm coming!," she screeched out of the driveway and disappeared far down the street and out of sight.

Chapter 15

"UH OH. IT'S still frozen," Mom said Thanksgiving morning when I came down for breakfast.

I rushed over to the sink, where she stood, poking the frozen turkey.

"You didn't leave it out?" I said. It was rock solid.

"Leave it out where?"

"I thought you said you knew how to do this."

"I do!" Mom stammered like a child. "I just didn't realize how…." She filled the sink with hot water. "I thought it needed to be kept cold all night. But maybe if we turn it and keep adding water, it'll thaw."

Her mouth was pursed. Little vertical lines like stitches had formed in the area above her top lip. Grandma had those same lines, probably from pursing her lips when she concentrated, but Mom wasn't exactly concentrating on making a great Thanksgiving turkey. I couldn't believe she didn't fess up about not knowing how to cook it.

After five minutes of hot water, she said, "We can't do this all day. We'll go crazy. Let's put this thing in the tub."

I stared at her. "Mom."

"This'll work. I know it will." She wrapped a dishtowel around the turkey like that episode of "I Love Lucy" when Lucy, returning from France, pretended the wrapped hunk of cheese she'd brought on the plane was her baby.

In the upstairs bathroom that Blaire and I shared, Mom said, "Here. Hold this," and I held the frozen bird, which was hard but slightly soft in places from the quick douse in the kitchen sink.

She turned on the tub faucet and water rushed out. Usually at that point in the day, the aroma of roasting turkey would be drifting through the up-stairs hallway and into our bedroom, so tempting that I'd have to go down-stairs and have Dad carve off a small piece of crispy skin.

She placed it in the water, gave it a little scoot and it sailed across the tub.

"Good thing you're not interested in Jack Moyer," I said, going in front of the mirror.

"Why?"

I picked up the tube of Crest that was caked with dried toothpaste all around the opening from neither of us putting on the cap. "Because he probably expects turkey."

She flicked her hand. "Oh he doesn't care."

I tore off the hunk of dried Crest, which was gooey inside, like a jelly donut. "How do you know? Did you ask him?"

"I think he'll understand, Martie. I'm not too worried."

Now she was acting way too familiar with him. *Oh he won't care.*

I tossed the tube back on the sink, which was wet from the leaky fau-cets. I peered into my reflection and stared at it so long that my eyes stung. Dad would take an onion, a celery stalk and a few tomatoes and turn it into spaghetti sauce. He figured out things. He just did it.

My mind scanned the contents of our fridge. Two days ago, Mom had bought tons of groceries, preparing for Danny's arrival.

"Danny might like this cereal," she'd said at the store. And "Danny'll probably like a nice big hamburger while he's here."

I turned to Mom who sat on the edge of the tub, poking and turning the turkey. "I'll make tacos. I think we have the ingredients."

"No, no," Mom said. "Let's see what happens with this guy."

"Mom. Nothing's happening with this guy. He's frozen solid."

We both gazed at the tub in complete silence as if we were at a memorial service, viewing a casket.

"He was a good turkey," I said in a solemn tone.

Mom laughed. It was her dinner party laugh, the one Blaire and I could hear above all the other dinner guests when we were younger. The casual sound of it filled me with a deep longing for the way things used to be—the four of us, not a perfect family, but a family whose dad maybe didn't think about our futures but definitely thought about the present.

"We can order Chinese food," Mom said.

"On Thanks*giv*ing? *No!*"

I turned away from her and rushed down the stairs, swinging open the fridge.

"Okay. Cheese," I said to myself, tossing the orange block on the counter. My hand grabbed a quarter head of Romaine lettuce. "Lettuce."

Good thing she'd bought ground beef. Danny wouldn't be able to have his hamburger, but he'd live.

"You know what?"' Mom said in the doorway, holding the bird in her arms. "We'll all go out and have a nice meal so no one has to cook."

"What are you planning on doing with that?"

"This? Defrost it, I suppose. Have it another night. I'll put it in the downstairs fridge."

I surveyed the food items on the counter. "Okay, so we're good with taco stuff. We have enough."

"Martie, I can't have you cook the whole meal."

"I want to," I said, nodding. "I really do."

Mom's chin was doing that shaky thing that meant she was about to cry.

"It'll be fun," I went on, realizing that we didn't have sour cream.

Mom deposited the turkey back in the sink and rushed toward me, burying her face in the crook of my neck the same way I used to do in hers when I couldn't bear getting on the bus to go to kindergarten.

"It's okay," I said, feeling the smallness of her in my arms. Her hair had gone one day too long and now a muskiness drifted up my nostrils.

"I ruined it," she blurted out. "I ruined the whole thing."

"Mom, no. You didn't."

My neck was wet from her warm tears, which gave me this weird feeling for a second like I was holding *me*. But it was Mom.

"You're the only one I have," she whispered, leaning into me as if she were about to collapse. "The only one who hasn't left me."

I hadn't thought of it that way, but she was right. Dad had left all of us, but Blaire had also left Mom, so now it was all me. The savior.

I felt suffocated just thinking about it.

———

I browned and salted the beef while Blaire and Danny watched a football game on T.V. Julie arrived, carrying two homemade apple pies and wearing a loose black dress and a long black sweater on top of that. She meandered around the kitchen, picking at the cheese and cracker tray that I'd prepared earlier.

"I tell you one thing," Julie said. "The world is a different place without your father. A place I don't like half as much, by the way." It was weird, her small, squinty eyes were kind of like Dad's. I'd never noticed that before. Maybe pieces of him were scattered all over the place and I just needed to start looking for them.

My hand reached into the bag of Fritoes, which Blaire and Danny had bought yesterday, and I ate them one by one as I stirred the meat. Like Dad, I felt comfortable standing at the stove, moving food around in a pan.

"Did your mom tell you about the little trip we're taking?"

A Frito poked the inside of my cheek. "Where?" I didn't want her going away. What if the plane crashed? "When?"

"Chicago. After New Years. Just a little ladies weekend."

"How're you getting there?"

"Driving."

I nodded, but my ears were blocked. All I could think about was getting a phone call from the hospital saying that Mom had died.

Pressing my palm against my heart, I counted the beats. *Palpitations are feelings or sensations that your heart is pounding or racing. They can be felt in your chest, throat or neck.*

I was such a baby. I hated how scared I was all the time. The bad thing in our lives had already happened. There was no way that God or whoever controlled everything would take Mom, too.

"Martie?" Julie said. "Earth to Martie."

"He's here!" Mom called from the front hall.

I rushed to the living room window and pushed aside the curtain. Jack Moyer walked with a purpose across the driveway like he had important things to do. Maybe it was the white shirt, yellow tie and navy overcoat.

Before Mom swung open the door, she locked eyes with me. A smear of foundation on her temple hadn't been rubbed in and looked as orange as Allie's tanning lotion. I imagined her confessing that Jack Moyer was her boyfriend and that they planned on getting married.

"Let's just get through this," she whispered instead. "That's all we have to do."

I nodded and felt so relieved I wanted to cry.

Cold air and cologne rushed in as Jack Moyer stood on our Welcome mat, smiling with perfect teeth except for the flash of silver somewhere in the back of his mouth. Dad's eyes turned small and dark by the day's end, but Mr. Moyer's were bright and clear like he could see for miles.

"This is Martie," Mom said, her hand on the small of my back, pushing me slightly toward him like I was supposed to hug him. "She's my baby."

"So *this* is Martie." Like he'd heard all about me. "How's the move been?"

I shrugged. "Okay." I glanced at Mom's left hand where she still wore her gold wedding band.

"Here, let me take your coat," Mom said.

"My folks moved me when I was about your age," he said, handing Mom his coat like she was his assistant. "Boy was I mad." Every time he moved, a wave of cologne came my way.

"Martie's my easy one," Mom whispered. "She's good at trying new things."

"Wisconsin's a solid place," he said like he alone represented the entire state. "It'll take good care of you."

He was trying to impress me. Clearly. Or maybe he was just being "attentive." I felt like saying, "My mom's not available, okay?"

"Come in. Please," Mom said. "It's too drafty in this hall. I need to weather strip that door." She grabbed Blaire, who was on her way upstairs, and introduced her. After shaking hands with him, Blaire eyed me like, Do you *smell* that?

"Beautiful family," he said, his eyes going from me to Blaire to Mom and back again. It was a little weird.

He followed Mom into the living room, which she'd tidied up earlier by fluffing couch pillows and stashing her real estate folders in her desk.

"What a view," he said, stopping to face the bay window.

Blaire and I locked eyes. She made a secretive fanning gesture to her nose like "P.U!" I pressed my lips together so hard that it hurt.

We all stood there, taking in the view. It was kind of cool that we could point from the edge of our backyard and say, "That's Michigan!" even though today Michigan was nothing more than a dark green sliver.

"The lake is stunning," Mr. Moyer said, breaking the silence. "Just stunning."

That time I laughed. I couldn't help it. Then I tried to cover it up by acting like it was a cough.

"I hope no one had their hearts set on turkey," Mom said, readjusting her necklace. "Martie and I had a little, uh, unfortunate incident with the—"

"It didn't thaw," I explained, and shuffled back to the kitchen where Blaire and Julie stood at the counter, whispering.

I stirred the ground beef a little more, then tasted it. Bland. In the spice rack I found chili powder. *Hot!* the label said. Perfect. I shook the container once and the entire contents of the bottle dumped out, forming a mound on top of the beef.

"Shit!" I whispered, trying to spoon out the excess.

"Mmm," Julie said, peering over my shoulder and chewing a piece of cheese that smelled like dirty feet. "Smells good."

"I just messed up the whole thing," I said, close to tears.

"Oh, I'm sure it's wonderful."

"Blaire," Mom called. "Bring the white wine out here, won't you?"

"What the hell? She can't get it herself?"

"I'll do it." I left the ruined meat and grabbed the bottle.

"I'll come with you," Julie said, linking her arm through mine. Could she ever *not* touch people?

I held the bottle in one hand, remembering my parents' parties, where Blaire and I weaved between the guests, offering cheese-covered olives and carafes of wine.

"Thank you, Martie," Mr. Moyer said when I held out the bottle. He picked up his glass and held it while I poured. *Glunkglunkglunk* It was the sound of my parents in the screened-in porch before dinner, watching that day's recap of the Watergate hearings.

"So how're you liking the Midwest?"

I stopped pouring when I got an inch from the top of his glass. "It's good."

"People treating you okay?"

"Uh huh."

The three of them stared at me like they were waiting for a show to begin. Or maybe they were counting the zits on my forehead.

Mom, clearly sensing my discomfort, clapped her hands once and said, "I know! Let's do Wisconsin facts!"

"Now?" I said.

She turned to Jack. "Julie gave us a fact book that Martie's taken quite a liking to."

"Facts such as…?" His thick dark eyebrows reminded me of caterpillars.

"Ahmmm…." I glanced out the window, trying to think. "Such as…" Waves slapped against the seawall next door and crashed into the air. I turned back to him. "Such as: Wisconsin has the highest number of Polish immigrants of any other state."

He winked at Mom like, *She's a cute puppy. She does tricks.*

I kicked into gear. "What's the University of Wisconsin's mascot?"

"Badger," he said.

"*Badger?*" Mom said. "Really?"

"Where's the original Barbie from?" I asked.

"Barbie? Are you kidding me?" Blaire said as she and Danny walked into the room, drinking Sprites that were probably spiked with vodka.

"I should know this," Julie said. "Does it start with a D?"

Jamie Holland

"Willows, Wisconsin," I told them. "What's Barbie's full name?"

"That's a tough one," Mom said. "Her full name? Was that ever written on the box?"

"*Willows*?" Julie was still stuck on the previous question. "Where the heck is that?" She squinted at the wall like soon a map of Wisconsin would appear.

Jack Moyer laughed. "Lived here my whole life and I had no idea Barbie was born here."

"Barbie Millicent Roberts," I told them. I loved being the one with the answers.

"Magnificent," he said, shaking his head and gazing out the window like he was admiring the love of his life. "A truly magnificent body of water."

That time I laughed and didn't even try to cover it up.

I'd cooked the tortillas too long and they crumbled into shards when we tried to fold them, so everyone ate with forks instead of their hands.

Julie raised her glass. "To the next great chef in the house!"

"Cheers to the wise owl," Blaire said. She sounded a little drunk.

Julie didn't drink from her glass; she held it there, looking at each of us. "After such a…heart-wrenching year, I just wanted to…"

A weight pressed down on me. Inside my head a tickertape streamed the words *Don't cry Don't cry Don't cry.*

"I'm so thankful for each one of you," she went on, her eyes glistening. "And I know if Steven were here today…"

I turned to Mom who was biting the inside of her cheek. Maybe she was preparing a toast in her head. All I wanted was to see Dad one more time, to feel his sure grasp on my shoulder, to breathe in the cedar smell of his sweaters and the faint Noxzema on his cheeks, but what I saw was a staticky image like how a T.V. screen looks without the antenna. Was that normal? To not be able to call up your dad's face?

Finally Julie sat down and wiped away her tears. "Please. Go ahead with thankfuls. Oh!" And she stood again. "I'm also thankful that Nixon is out of the White House."

Jack Moyer jumped in. "I'm thankful that Martie made tacos. I've never liked turkey." He flashed us a smile like he'd been waiting all night to share his admission.

Mom laughed way too loudly and shot me a glance. "Well, it's a good thing our little friend never thawed, isn't it, Martie?"

I was the only one she had. How was that possible? And what did it mean, exactly, for me? That I could never get mad at her?

Blaire kissed Danny on the cheek and said, "I'm thankful for Danny."

Danny said, "I'm thankful the Cowboys won."

Julie laughed. "Be careful. This is Packers territory."

Blaire and I locked eyes and I wondered if she was thinking about Dad's Redskins painting. I'd never forget staring into the vertical smears of burgundy and gold, trying to make out human shapes.

"I don't see one football player," I'd told Blaire.

"You're too literal," Blaire said. "You don't get art."

Mom put her elbow on the table, something she told us to never do, and sunk her chin in her hand, smiling in a far-off way.

Julie was quick to cock her head and put on her empathic face.

"Can someone please tell me how your father managed to get so much paint on him?" She shook her head, amused at the memory. "Legs, arms..."

"Ears," I threw in. "Hair."

Mom turned to her boss to include him in the story. "Then he'd go to the grocery store that way. Completely unaware."

"Soles of shoes," Blaire added, referring to the time he tracked red paint all the way through the kitchen.

"Oh! I could've killed him!" Mom said.

Bad choice of words, which I tried to cover up by saying, "Remember his snoring?" and immediately Blaire and I threw back our heads, opened our mouths and imitated Dad's strained inhale followed by the puffed cheeks that produced a small jet of air through slightly parted lips.

Mr. Moyer's face turned red like our demonstration had become too intimate for him.

"Oh it wasn't quite that bad," Mom said, clearly amused.

I wanted to go back and forth, weaving memory over memory until finally we'd hold in our hands a quilt of stories about him that one day would keep us warm.

"One more thankful," Blaire said.

We all turned to her. Mom's eyebrows rose in anticipation.

"I'm thankful I quit tennis." She picked up a triangle of hardened tortilla and swirled it in the leftover glob of Tabasco.

"What?" Mom said, squinting now. "You did what?"

Danny bit his lip and then reached for his Sprite.

"I want to be an artist," she said. "Like Dad."

"Yes, but..." Mom touched her throat and glanced at the lake as if for support.

"It's already done. I quit on Tuesday."

"Danny?" Mom said, grasping for answers. "Were you aware of this?"

"Why does it matter if he knew or not?" Blaire said. "It's my business."

"Babe," Danny said under his breath. "Take it easy."

"You love tennis," Mom said.

"I'm sick of it. I want to draw. And paint. That's all I want to do."

"You can play tennis *and* paint," Mom said. "Just because you're sick of one thing doesn't mean you have to—"

"Sounds like she doesn't want to play tennis anymore," Julie said, as if Mom needed a translator.

"Well, that's a big mistake," Mom said.

"Yeah, well," Blaire said, shoving another bite in her mouth. "You've made mistakes, too, so..." She eyed Mom like they shared some deep dark secret and right then I had the sickest thought: Mom murdered Dad. The idea flickered in front of me like a Fourth of July sparkler until it fell from my grasp and dunked into a bucket of water and everything turned dark again.

Chapter 16

Mrs. Neely asked to see me after class. She stood by her desk, crimson half-glasses perched on the end of her nose.

"Have a seat." In front of a full class, her mouth went up at the corners and her eyes danced behind her glasses, but today her red lips were pursed, her forehead creased in deep concentration.

"You need to start taking risks." She stared at me hard, like she was waiting for the words to sink into my skin. My pores. No. It was more than that. She saw all the way inside me to a place I'd only glimpsed.

A plant sat on her desk with light green tendrils that fell almost all the way to the floor.

"It's up to each one of us to get our stories out there in the world," she said.

"But what if I don't have a story?"

"You do. It's just a matter of peeling off the layers. Dredging it up."

Dredging it up from *where*? She made it sound like my story was trapped beneath the ocean floor.

"I used to write," I said, hopeful that maybe she'd count my old journal entries instead of my current homework assignments.

"Did you," she said, unimpressed. She even sighed a little.

I locked eyes with her and made myself not look away. Beyond the glasses and mascara, her eyes were green, like Mom's.

"I *am* trying," I said. "It's just…not a lot comes out."

"Write about your most painful memory."

She wanted me to write about Dad, but I couldn't. Not yet. I needed answers first. I needed to call that psychiatrist, too, and see if he knew anything.

"Don't be afraid of what you write," she said, leaning toward the plant and touching the soil with two fingers. "They're just words on a page."

Right. Just words on a page.

"Not to mention," she went on as she got up and retrieved the plastic water pitcher from the windowsill. "The exercise of writing can reap unexpected benefits."

"Like what?"

She poured a dribble and the dirt drank it up. She did that over and over, like little feedings, until the soil was dark and moist.

"You'll see."

⊷⊶

"Danny hasn't called once since he left," Blaire said as we pulled into our driveway. It was a week after Thanksgiving and now we took the Mustang to school each day even though the heat didn't work and you had to hit the dashboard to get the radio to work.

"He's probably just busy," I said. "You know, homework and all that."

Mrs. Neely expected six pages from me by the first day we got back from Christmas vacation. My most painful memory. I could start with the afternoon that everything changed, but all I remembered were snippets— Mom's real estate folders piled neatly on the kitchen table, Blaire's choked sobbing from the bathroom—and then the curtain went down and everything turned black.

Inside I grabbed the hunk of cheddar cheese and the sharpest knife I could find. *Wisconsin produces over 450 varieties, types and styles of nationally award-winning cheeses.*

Blaire sat at the table, going through the pile of mail that she'd brought in from the foyer, and I stood at the counter, shoving little shavings of cheese into my mouth. Early that morning, a light snowfall had dusted our grass and trees like confectioner's sugar, but now the sky was blue and the sun had melted the snow from the trees. I'd been waiting for a big snowfall that would freeze the lake in chunks and make thick, pointy icicles hang from doorways.

"Damnit!" She tossed the mail across the table and the envelopes slid almost all the way off the edge.

"Maybe his letter got lost in the mail." I plopped another piece of cheese in my mouth and let the tanginess settle on my tongue.

"No," she said, pacing the kitchen, a worry line indenting her forehead. "Something's wrong."

"Like what?"

"I don't know! That's what I'm saying! He's not like this!"

"Did you call him?"

"He's ignoring me. I know he is." She bit the side of her thumb. "I have to see him. I have to."

I thought of saying, "Maybe you could fly to Maryland on the witch's broomstick." Danny would laugh at that, but not Blaire. No way.

Upstairs I took out my composition book and tried to write, but my mind kept drifting to the psychiatrist. I told myself to write at least a page before I called him.

Maybe I'd write in a different voice. I could pretend I was the older Hanley girl, getting ready for the mall. I'd read so much about the case that I knew the exact route they took to get there. Before long, I could hear the sentences streaming out of her mouth and the excitement building as she approached the jewelry store where she'd buy a necklace for herself.

I wrote two pages, then rifled around in my sock drawer for the business card. His phone number was long distance, of course, but I'd make it a quick call and maybe it would never even show up on the bill.

I pushed the numbers. What if he said, "Oh yes, of course I remember him. I'm sorry that he chose to end his life." Or maybe he'd say, "Steven Wheeler? Who?"

Two rings. They sounded far away. I pictured a black phone on a clean desk. Maybe a few framed photos of a smiling wife and kids, no signs in their eyes of lingering suspicions after a family member's death. Normal funeral with open casket and final kisses on a cool forehead.

A click, like someone picking up. What was I doing calling a psychiatrist whose number I found in a random folder?

"Hello?" I said, twisting my fingers around the cord.

"I'm sorry," said the robotic female voice. "The number you're trying to reach has been disconnected." Then a high-pitched tone that assaulted my ears. "I'm sorry. The number you're trying to reach—"

"Oh shut up!" I yelled and slammed down the phone.

Blaire burst out of her room. "Jesus Christ, Martie! Some people are trying to sleep around here!"

"All you do is sleep!" I screamed at her and for once, I was the one to slam the door.

Chapter 17

WE SPENT CHRISTMAS Eve at a pathetic place called Rick's Food and Drink, which was decorated with tinsel and colored blinking lights. Dad would've hated it.

Mom, wearing way too much red lipstick, ordered fondue for the three of us, and a glass of wine for herself. "Girls, get something," she said. "Have something fun."

"Like alcohol?" Blaire said.

"Like 7-Up," she said. "Or Coke."

Outside the snow came down hard, coating sidewalks and bushes, cars and trees. I wanted to be in it, my arms stretched out to the sides, spinning round and round.

"I know this isn't perfect," she said to us as she cradled her wine glass in both hands like it was a bubble that could break at any moment. "I know it's not Christmas-y, but..." She glanced around. "It's kind of fun to be out, isn't it?"

"Fun?" Blaire said.

"I think it's stunning," I said, channeling Jack Moyer. "Just stunning."

Mom laughed.

Blaire rolled her eyes in a disgusted way like she couldn't stand the sight of us. I couldn't stand the sight of me, either. I hated that I hadn't even tried to find Dad's recipe for the veal stew he made every Christmas Eve. Yesterday Mom had said, "Let's go out for fondue," and, like the little pleaser, I nodded and went along with it. All I could tolerate was the slightest dip in the water before I crawled back under Mom's wing, too scared to speak up for fear of being tossed out of the nest forever.

The fondue arrived in a big red vat, three long thin forks on the side.

Mom picked up one and said, "So you just take one of these pieces of bread and dunk it right in." Her piece now dripped with light yellow cheese. "Go ahead, try it."

It tasted the way wine smelled except that the fondue was warm and thick. It coated my tongue.

"Blaire, let's try it," Mom said in that same camp counselor tone. "Come on. Take a fork."

But she was deep in her sketchbook, using the side of her pencil to shade in a lightning bolt.

"What *is* that?" I asked her. "And why do you always—"

She moved the book so that I couldn't see it. "Nothing."

My heart picked up a few beats. Lately it was happening when I wasn't even thinking about anything in particular. *The emergency warning signals of a heart attack include chest pain that travels to the arm, neck, jaw, back or shoulders. Crushing or squeezing pain. Chest pain, accompanied by a cold sweat.*

"It's a Wonderful Life" played on a television screen to the right of the bar. Over the years I'd seen the movie in fragments but never from beginning to end. In one scene George Bailey trudged through the snow, crazed and desperate, and in another he appeared ecstatic as he held his curly-haired daughter in his arms. I never saw the scenes that connected the two, the ones that showed how he got from one place to another.

To the left of the bar was another T.V. *1974* was written in big letters, and then a series of photos flashed on the screen. Patty Hearst, Muhammad Ali, Nixon on the helicopter, a scene from "The Sting," the Watergate building, and then a bunch of the guys who'd testified—Ehrlichman, Haldemann, Dean, Mitchell. Ehrlichman had always scared me—his oily skin and receding hairline, his dark raised eyebrow. None of them looked trustworthy.

"I know!" Mom said. "Let's play Ghost!"

"Why do you always have to play these *stupid* games?" Blaire mumbled.

Mom, clenching her teeth, said, "Martie, you start. You're good at this game."

We used to play it when the four of us drove to Florida in the station wagon.

"Okay," I said. "S." I placed a small square of bread on my tongue like it was communion.

Ghost was a spelling game. One person said a letter and the next person added to it and it kept going around like that until we'd spelled a word. There weren't really any rules—I didn't even know where we'd come up with the game or why it was called Ghost.

"L" Mom said, eager for the next letter.

My personal goal was to think of long words—twelve, fifteen letters— and hope that, as we went around the circle, each of us tacking on a new let- ter that, in the end, we'd end up with a real word, not just a jumble of random letters. I imagined the letters going round and round like mesh, wrapping around our three bodies, holding us together no matter what.

But when it was Blaire's turn, she grabbed her coat with the broken zip- per and said, "I'm leaving."

"Well, you're not going alone," Mom said and raised her arm for the check. Now I was pissed at Blaire for ruining a nice moment.

"Why did you have to do that?" I asked her as we headed for the door.

"You really want to sit there and play some stupid spelling game?"

"It's better than being at home!"

"Then *stay* if you want!"

The winter air stung my cheeks. I breathed in snowflakes and they went straight up my nose, numbing my brain. When we got home, I'd take out my composition book and write how horrible Christmas Eve was and what a loser I was for not sticking up for myself.

Mom walked quickly in front of us, her heels knocking against the partly shoveled sidewalk.

She swung open the car door, got in and slammed it shut. Must've been ten below inside the car.

"I'm *trying*," she said. "I don't know what else to do." Her breath tumbled out in clouds that hung briefly in the air, then disappeared.

She started the ignition and the vents blasted out cold air. The radio was turned on low, but I could hear a man singing, "Have a Holly Jolly Christmas."

The windshield wipers swept away the flurries, but a second later, they returned. At the stop sign, a streetlight shone on her face. Her lipstick had worn off.

"I can't do this anymore." She stepped on the accelerator and we swerved for a second before straightening out.

"Maybe you should slow down," I said.

"You don't understand!"

I flinched at her tone.

"You don't have a father!"

The freezing air rushing out of the vents fogged my glasses. I slapped at the controls, trying to find the warmth.

"And there's no guarantee that you'll be okay."

"What do you mean, 'there's no...'?" I asked in a small voice.

"Life isn't fair! Nothing's turned out the way I thought it would!" She flung out the words like they were old, unwanted shoes from the back of her closet.

I glanced back at Blaire, who faced the window, stone-faced, like she'd blocked out Mom's voice.

On Lake Drive, tall houses sat on cliffs. One was boarded up with a sign that said, "Condemned Property." Allie had told me that houses fell in the lake from erosion. She said people who lived on the water needed sea walls, which we didn't have.

We turned down our street. Descending the hill was like sinking into a hole. Soon we were at our house, which was so quiet and dark I wanted to scream. Not even the Christmas tree lights were on. I wondered what Tommy was doing at that moment. Probably watching T.V. There was no way that he or Allie had a pit in their stomach on Christmas Eve.

Mom drove the car into the garage and put it in Park. The headlights flashed against the wall, briefly spotlighting the shovel and rake that leaned against it.

She turned off the ignition and gazed into the windshield where a crack fell all the way down the center of the glass like a run in a pair of L'eggs pantyhose. "A father dying is…" She shook her head. "It'll affect you…forever. And the repercussions… You just have no idea…"

She'd never said any of that before, not even after he'd died. Never had she talked about what kind of effect it would have on us. And it sounded like she knew exactly what the repercussions were. Stupidly, I'd assumed that everything eventually would be okay. That we'd learn how to live without him. But now she made it sound like we'd spend the rest of our lives staggering around like zombies, unable to function.

"Carol Specter was right," Mom said, opening her door. "It doesn't go away. But it doesn't get easier. That's where she was wrong."

◆◆◆

Mom retreated to her bedroom and closed the door. Blaire stood in the foyer, rifling through last week's mail, probably still searching for a letter from Danny. I could hear the snow landing on the windows, a soft whispery sound that made me want to scream.

I opened the back door and went outside. The snow glittered. I bent down and fluffed it up in the air like a kid at low tide. My fingertips burned. I didn't care. I did it again and again and then made a snowball, attempting to throw it at Mom's window, but I was terrible at throwing and it fell before it even reached the house.

I turned and faced the lake, which, in the dark, looked frozen. Or maybe part of it had frozen. I stared into the vast nothingness, thinking of Dad at the ocean's edge, gazing at everything and nothing at the same time.

The Hanley girls would miss Christmas. I couldn't stand not knowing if they were dead or alive.

"Where *are* you?" I yelled into the cold air, stomping my foot in the snow.

I squeezed my eyes shut, *Please be alive, please be alive,* and when they opened, I watched the flurries fall down on me like stars from heaven.

Chapter 18

"IS THIS CHARACTER *you*?" Mrs. Neely asked me the day after I proudly handed in ten pages.

I shook my head. "It's someone else. Someone whose voice I'm imagining."

Behind her thick glasses, her eyes twinkled. "And what made you focus on someone other than yourself?"

She seemed intrigued. Maybe I'd successfully dredged up my story.

"Well," I started. "I've thought about these girls a *lot*. So I feel like I kind of *was* them. I mean, was *her*. The older one."

"Mmm."

"So I just imagined the whole thing. Like that she was thinking about buying a necklace at the mall and that she and her sister were talking about how mad they were that their dad wouldn't let them get their ears pierced."

"I'm still unclear about one part of this," she said.

I nodded. "Which part?"

"When the assignment was specifically to write about your*self* and no one else, then why did you feel you were entitled to not do that?"

Oh come *on*. Why was she being so inflexible? I was writing, wasn't I? Wasn't that the whole point?

"I thought it would be okay since I—"

"Since you what? Lost your father?"

My stomach dropped. "What?"

"Being in the club doesn't give you creative license. It doesn't mean you get to freely translate homework into anything you want it to be."

"How did you know about my dad?"

She leaned forward. "What matters is that you write about *your* self. Not someone else's self. And the only way you can do that is by reaching deep inside."

"But—" I was about to cry. How did she expect me to go deep? I needed a jackhammer to break through myself.

"I recognize that you tried. But now you need to go back to the drawing board."

"So all the writing I did is just…wasted?"

"It's never wasted." She slid a pile of papers in front of her like she was eager to get back to work.

"So what am I supposed to do now?"

Her glare said it all: *Write about the painful memory, you idiot.*

After a long disapproving frown, she slid her glasses up her nose and began reading other students' deep thoughts.

⊷⊷

At home I went straight up the staircase, determined to write something decent about *my* self. I threw my backpack on my bed and stood there for a second, staring at the Robert Redford picture tacked to my bulletin board. A snipping sound came from behind the bathroom door. Like scissors cutting fabric.

I tiptoed to the hallway. Definitely scissors. Maybe Blaire was turning jeans into cut-offs, getting ready for spring, although I had the feeling that warmer weather would never come.

I knocked. "Blaire?"

"What." More snipping.

"Can I…" and usually I wouldn't have barged in, but something told me to open the door.

Blaire stood at the sink, cutting her hair up to her ears.

"No!" I reached for the scissors and the blade scraped my palm.

A thin line of blood rose up and I wiped it away. "Why are you *doing* that?"

Pieces dropped to the white bathroom rug and lay there—twelve-inch clumps, maybe fifteen.

"Stop it!" I said. "Don't do that!" But it kept falling—in the sink, on the floor—like she couldn't stop herself. I lunged again for the scissors, but she held them out of reach the same way she did with her sketchbook when I asked her why she drew the lightning bolts.

In seconds her hair turned short and spiky. She snipped the back of her head like she was clipping grass.

"Why are you *doing* that?" I yelled. I hated the way she looked. Short hair made her head look tiny and triangular, like an alien.

The blonde streak, which was barely blonde anymore, lay limp by her feet. She bent down, grabbed the mass and flung it in the trash. When she stood up again, the snipping continued. I couldn't stand the sound.

Back in my room, I stood at my desk where the Merck Manual and the Hanley binder sat, side by side, like bibles. My eyes went back and forth from one to the other until I reached for the book and read *Palpitations are feelings or sensations that your heart is pounding or racing. They can be felt in your chest, throat or neck.* The last sentence in the paragraph sounded like it was straight out of a fortune cookie. *You may have an unpleasant awareness of your own heartbeat.*

I pushed away the book and opened my denim binder to the middle. A photo of the sisters smiled at me—their sweet summer faces squinting in the sun. If they lived through their kidnapping, they'd never get over it. They'd never trust anyone again.

Chapter 19

IN THE MORNING my eyes were puffy. The zit cream had dried on my skin, masking the pimples and, just as I had every morning for as long as I could remember, I stood, bent over the sink, lathering my face, hoping that when I rinsed and dried it, my forehead would be clear.

It was just as bad as yesterday and the day before. I had a creeping feeling that it would always be that way, that me obsessively covering my forehead each night would never result in clear skin. Ever. What made me think that some stupid cream mixed with a few drops of toner would destroy my zits? Why hadn't I ever thought to just stop using it altogether? They were pores, after all—why wasn't I letting them breathe like Mom had taught me?

I put on tan cords and a light blue button down shirt that I left untucked. I grabbed my backpack and headed for Mom's room. She scuttled around, packing the last of her clothes in a small brown suitcase that had once belonged to her mom. Each time she set a shirt or a pair of pantyhose in the bag, she placed her hands on it, said, "Okay," and went to the bureau for more.

"When are you coming back?" I asked her.

She drew in a deep breath. "I shouldn't even be going."

"What do you mean?"

"Your sister," was all she said as she tucked a handful of underwear along the edges of the suitcase.

"She'll be fine," I said. "It's just a haircut." But I knew it was more than a haircut; I just didn't know *what* exactly.

Mom sighed. "I need to find her a psychiatrist."

My ears perked up. "Really?"

"She'll refuse to go, but she needs to talk to someone." Into the bag went her nightgown, which she balled into a corner.

"I'll go if she doesn't."

"No, no. She'll go." She zipped her bag and glanced at her gold watch that hung loose from her wrist like a bracelet. "Julie said she'd be here by now."

"Maybe I should go, too."

"You're not coming to Chicago with us."

"To the psychiatrist," I said.

Mom shot me that *Stop being a hypochondriac* look. "There's nothing wrong with you, Martie."

I tore a loose thread from the bottom of my shirt. "But what if there is?"

"Do you *want* to have something wrong with you? Because you're acting like you do."

I glanced down at the nail polish stain. I couldn't believe her scrubbing had made such a mess. "No. I just…"

She rushed into the bathroom and returned with her deodorant, which she slipped into her purse. So many little movements. From here to there and back again a million times.

"Mom?"

She grabbed the leather handle and pulled the suitcase to the floor.

"What if you die?"

"Oh for God's sake, Martie. Please don't ask that. Not now."

"Just what if? I mean, who would we live with?" My fingertips went to my forehead, feeling the craters.

"Julie."

"But what if something happens to Julie?" I said.

"You'll go with her father's other sister, I suppose," she said. "Aunt Lillian."

My eyes narrowed. "Aunt Lillian who we haven't seen in about ten years?" Actually she'd been at the funeral, but she scared me. Her pale face and dark red lipstick. And the way she sat in the back of the church with her lips pursed, shaking her head each time I glanced her way.

"Isn't there someone else?" I said.

"Why don't *you* think of someone?" But she didn't wait for me to rattle off a list and I didn't know who I'd choose anyway—Robin's mom? Mrs. Neely?

She dragged her suitcase across the carpet and lugged it down the stairs where Blaire sat on the bottom step digging through her backpack. Each time I saw her hair it was like a shock all over again.

"I'll have someone check on you two while I'm gone," Mom said, peering out the window that looked out onto the driveway.

"We don't need that." Blaire stood, wearing torn jeans and a flannel shirt that was about two sizes too big. "We'll be fine."

If she'd gone to a hair salon, then maybe someone could've made her look okay, but since she'd cut it all off herself, it was uneven and blunt at the same time, flicking out in the weirdest ways.

In the kitchen Mom collected the last of her things—sunglasses, keys—then said, "Let me write down the hotel number just in case..." She felt around in her purse and came up with a ballpoint pen and a scrap of paper.

"I've got my license," Blaire said. "So if anything happens..."

"Like what?" I said. "What would happen?" I had a pang in my stomach and I wanted to hold on to the hem of Mom's coat like I used to do.

After she scribbled on the piece of paper, she handed it to Blaire, who shoved it in her front pocket.

Outside a car honked. Julie's car. From the same window where I watched Jack Moyer walk confidently toward our house, I witnessed Mom slip on our front walkway, catch herself, then disappear safely inside the car.

Five minutes after she left, Blaire lit a cigarette.

"Oh don't freak out," she said to me. Smoke rushed out of her nostrils like hot dragon breath.

"You're inhaling smoke," I said. "It's not exactly good for you."

"We need to go," she said. She grabbed her coat, slid her feet into boots and grabbed her backpack. I closed the door behind us and locked the door. The cold air swirled like a cyclone, ripping off the layers of my skin.

"Danny's coming tonight," Blaire said in the freezing car.

"*Here?*" I wanted to say, *I thought he hadn't written or called.*

"He's interviewing at Purdue. And trying out for basketball." She inhaled one more time, opened her door partway and tossed the cigarette on top of a mound of snow. I knew it would burn out, but I wanted to see that happen with my own eyes because now I'd go to school all worried that the stub had rolled all the way to the garage and lit up the house.

Blaire turned the key and the car coughed and sputtered and then started.

"Did you tell him about your hair?" I said, rubbing my hands together to get them warm.

She shifted into Drive. "Nope."

"Won't he be kind of freaked out?"

She turned onto the street and drove away from our house. "You're just like Mom. Focusing on how everything looks."

Well, yeah. In her case, I *was* focusing on how she looked because she looked horrible.

⬥⬥

"How's Chicago?" I asked Mom that night. I was in her room, eating the last piece of Celeste pizza and flipping the channels of the black and white T.V.

"It's very windy right now," she said.

"Have you seen the lake?"

"I'm looking at it right now."

I went to Mom's window. White lawn, dark lake. I couldn't even remember what the backyard looked like in warm weather.

"Remember the way the ocean would get in Florida before a storm?" she said. "All those white caps? It's like that here."

I liked that we could look at the same body of water at the same time even though we were in two different states.

"You know what I heard today?" she said.

"What?"

"On a clear day, if you stand on top of the Sears Tower, you can see Michigan, Wisconsin, Illinois and Indiana."

"Do they let people stand up there?"

"Maybe. I don't know."

I returned to her bed and let myself fall back on her pillows. I pictured Mom small as a Barbie doll, teetering on top of that tall building.

"How's Blaire?"

"Fine."

"You have the number here, right?"

"Uh huh."

"If she does something else impulsive like cutting off all her hair, you call me." I didn't like the word "impulsive." Dad was impulsive and he was dead now.

I heard a car pull into our driveway and then the rush of Blaire's feet down the staircase.

"Did you hear me?" Mom said.

"Yup." I rose up from the bed and looked down at Danny's car. "I'll call you. I promise."

After hanging up, I rushed to the top of the stairs and spied on them. Blaire had thrown herself on him and he'd wrapped his arms around her, but it wasn't like that hug from the airport when I felt all jealous watching them.

He let go of her quicker than normal and squinted at her hair like it crawled with lice. "Why would you do this?"

Blaire ran her fingers through what was left of it and shrugged. "I just felt like it."

He stepped away. "Jesus, Blaire."

"What?" she said, moving toward him. "I'm still *me*. *God*. It's just *hair*." She sounded small, though, like she was calling to him from inside a deep well.

———

"We're getting married," Blaire said in the morning as she waited by the toaster. Her eyes were bright, her cheeks flushed like she'd just come in from the cold. She wore a yellow Adidas t-shirt and the blue warm-up pants she once wore for tennis. Sharp tufts of hair stuck out of her scalp.

"*Now?*" I said, grabbing the milk.

"Not *now*," she said. "Maybe after college. Like *right* after."

Two English muffins popped up and she grabbed them, tossing the two halves on a plate and cutting through a stick of butter.

I poured Raisin Bran in my bowl. It looked like crushed up leaves. I hated thinking about Blaire getting married and moving away.

She took out a tray and put the plate on it, along with two glasses of orange juice. It was the way we'd arrange the breakfast-in-bed tray for Mother's and Father's Day. Dad always made eggs with sliced tomatoes on the side and a sprig of parsley on top. Mom's specialty was fresh croissants from the bakery on Chevy Chase Circle.

I glanced at my watch with one hand and poured milk on my cereal with the other. "We need to go in like ten minutes."

She picked up the tray. "I'm not going."

I scowled at her like a disapproving teacher. "Blaire."

She mocked me. "'Martie.'"

"So you're just gonna drop out of school and waste your life away?"

She carried the tray toward the doorway. "Yup. That's exactly what I plan on doing."

But when I got home from school, she was facedown on the living room carpet, wearing the same clothes as that morning.

"What happened?" I rushed over to her. Was it Mom? A car crash?

"He's...not..." Blaire's voice shook and trembled like she had the hiccups. "...in...love with me..."

I let go of my back pack, relieved it was only about Danny and not about something awful that had happened to Mom. "I'm sure he's in love with you."

She lifted her head. "No!" Her face was red, her eyelids swollen. "He said I've changed and that he doesn't think we should..." Her head fell to the carpet.

The phone rang. I grabbed it. "Hello?"

No one spoke immediately and I thought, Maybe it's Dad—not Dad coming back from the dead, but maybe he never even died. A new theory unfolded in my mind: Mom and Dad had wanted to divorce, but they couldn't bear to do it so they faked his death. Or maybe he was back in Spain where he'd learned how to paint in his twenties.

A woman with a high-pitched voice asked for my mom. Probably a potential client.

"Could you please have her call Helen Bennett at Jefferson High?"

"Yes," I said, eying Blaire who lay, slumped, like a wounded seal who'd washed ashore. "May I tell her what this in reference to?"

Usually Blaire would've rolled her eyes at me like, *What do you think you are—a receptionist?*

"Just have her call, please."

I hung up. Probably the attendance lady at her school.

From the floor, Blaire whispered, "He said he'd never, ever leave me."

"You guys have gotten in fights before," I reminded her. "You'll be fine."

"I *won't* be fine! You don't understand! I can't live without him!"

I dropped to the carpet next to her. "Danny loves you," I said, placing my hand on her trembling back. "Maybe he just got in a weird mood."

She shook her head. "No!"

Her back felt bony, as if she'd withered away between that morning and the afternoon. Danny would fix it. He'd call later and fix everything.

Chapter 20

IN THE MORNING all of Blaire's bureau drawers were pulled opened—t-shirts and bras flung here and there like she'd rifled through every item in a hopeless search. The only thing that wasn't all disorganized were the mason jars on her windowsill where she kept her paintbrushes.

She flew out of the closet with a sweatshirt and stuffed it in her backpack.

"What're you doing?" I said.

"Going to see him. You were right. We've gotten in other fights. This is just a little argument."

"You're going all the way to *Indiana?*" Why did she have to be so extreme? "How will you get there?"

"The Mustang."

"No! You'll freeze to death."

"I'll be fine. It's not that far."

She swished her hand inside her backpack like she was trying to grab onto a lost item in murky water.

"Are you sure he's still there?"

She pulled out her wallet and shoved it in a zippered pocket. "Yup. He's hanging out with the basketball team for like two more days."

"What about Mom? Aren't you gonna tell her?"

"No."

My chest tightened. Impulsive? Yes. Would I call Mom? Not sure. If Blaire went to Purdue and came back quickly, there'd be no reason to let her know.

"You need to come back today," I said from her doorway.

"That's not enough time." She threw her bag over her shoulder and brushed past me as she went down the stairs.

She opened the front door. The cold flew in like a thousand sharp knives. I grabbed my coat and backpack and followed her outside even though I hadn't even brushed my hair or teeth. "You can't do this!" I said, nearly slipping on the front path. "You can't leave me!"

She got to the Mustang and took out her keys. "I'll be back tomorrow. You'll be fine."

"No I won't! I can't stay here alone!"

She swung open the door. I got in the passenger seat and breathed in gasoline.

After she turned the key in the ignition, the engine sputtered, then died out. "Crap!" She pumped the accelerator up and down. The car kept cranking and cranking and not starting. I wanted her to flood the engine. I didn't even know what that meant, but I knew that a person wouldn't be able to drive all those miles with a flooded engine.

She hit the steering wheel with both fists. "Damnit!" She dug into her bag and came up with a cigarette, which she stuck between her lips. She punched in the lighter that Dad used back when he smoked. It popped out and she pressed it against the tip until it lit.

"You can't take this car! It's way too dangerous. And stop smoking!" I grabbed at the cigarette, but she held it out of my reach.

"The car works," she said. "It'll start in a minute."

"You'll freeze to death."

She inhaled and a long stream of smoke shot out of her mouth. It kept coming even after she'd blown it out. I pictured a thick grey swirl wrapping around her lungs like a snake.

"What if I never come back?" she said, smiling in an eerie way, staring out the windshield. "What if I just leave here and Danny and I start a whole new life together somewhere else?"

"Don't say that."

"Why?"

"Because you can't." I zipped my ski jacket. "You can't just leave like that."

What I wanted to say was, *I thought Danny wasn't in love with you anymore.*

She cleared her throat and reached for her keys that dangled from the ignition. The engine coughed and finally started.

"Thank God," she said.

We drove in silence. I hated that the three of us would soon be in three different states.

In front of my school, she took out a folded map from her bag, tossed it on the dashboard and said, "Okay."

"Okay what?"

"You need to get out."

I shoved my frozen hands into my coat pockets. My toes and fingertips felt numb.

She looked at me like a bored bus driver. "Martie."

Usually I'd throw that same expression back at her, say, "Blaire," until the corners of her mouth lifted, but neither of us was in a joking mood.

"The sooner I leave, the sooner I'll be back." She turned on the radio to static, then hit the dashboard and Bob Segar's gravelly voice filled the car.

The fact was, there was nothing I could do about it. She'd stepped over the bridge and now she was on the other side. And every time I threw her a line, she flicked it away like she'd rather swim further into the dark sea.

Chapter 21

AT LUNCH ALLIE and I went to the library to look up the amount of time it took to drive from our house to Purdue (four hours). Then I pulled out the atlas and opened to one of the Midwest pages.

"She's probably already there," I whispered, my finger tracing the curved path from Milwaukee to Lafayette. "It's weird. You have to go up and then down all that way."

"Mmhm." Allie sucked on a handful of M&Ms.

"That's a ton of driving," I said. "Especially in an older car."

"My dad always says that the older cars hold up much better than new ones."

I looked up. "But what if she skids on the ice? She doesn't even have snow tires."

"Some cars don't need them. Plus the highways are plowed," she said as if she herself plowed them that morning. "D'you have any information about the car? It might say something about it not needing snow tires or something."

I nodded. But what would that do? Relieve me for two seconds? In no time, I'd be back to picturing the car in a ditch.

"Or maybe research the type of tires? See what they say about them?"

"You think I know the *type* of tires? Are you serious?"

"I don't know. My dad's always talking about tires."

"But isn't it all about the actual car and not necessarily the tires?"

"I think it's the brake system."

I sighed. "There's no brake system. The car's for, like, driving to get ice cream on a hot day."

I closed the atlas. "I can't be*lieve* she left like that."

"She'll be back. I know she will."

I made myself focus on Allie's mole—the slightly irregular shape that I'd always thought was a perfect circle, the dark color that for months I'd thought was much lighter. How could I've thought I'd seen something that so clearly was not the way it actually was?

"I'd stay with you, but I've got a swim meet at six-thirty."

Allie's eyes were warm and brown, like melted chocolate. Perfect almonds. What was it about looking into a person's eyes that made you want to turn away? Turn away or cry.

⟞⟝

Shelly Stires sat alone on the empty bus, applying lip smacker. Bathed in the late afternoon light, she looked almost angelic—her glossy hair and shimmery mouth, the rosy cheeks and perfect skin. If she weren't so annoying, it would've been nice to be friends, mostly because we lived so close to one another.

"Hey Shelly," I said.

She didn't say a word. She put the cap on the lip smacker, crossed her arms like she was cold and turned away from me.

"Hi," I said, louder that time.

Nothing.

The bus lunged forward and I lost my footing and nearly fell on her.

"Find a seat," the bus driver called to me.

"Your sister's a freak," Shelly finally said, just barely glancing at me.

My eyes narrowed.

"She's at Susan's like, all the time."

I reached my hand out to the seatback in front of her to steady myself.

"I've heard things," she said.

"Like what?" Why was I even talking to her?

"Like that she's just as weird as Susan. That something's like wrong with her and she's—"

Usually I would've taken it. I would've swallowed the words and slunk away quietly, but I didn't want to be that person anymore who didn't make waves, the one who smiled primly while screaming inside.

"I've heard things, too," I started. "Like that you're in love with Tommy Lattiker and you flirt with him constantly, but you know what? He can't stand the sight of you. He's just too nice to say anything."

Triumphant, I floated past her and parked myself in an empty seat about five rows in back of her. My heart pounded—a good pounding, not the scared *I'm having a heart attack* kind.

The bus stopped and did its three-point turn at the witch's house. For once the faces didn't send a chill to my bones.

The doors opened and before Shelly got off, she yelled back at me. "If Tommy doesn't like me, then how come he asked me out? Huh?"

I wanted to yell back at her, but she'd already trotted down the steps and now she was walking, looking up at me with that self-satisfied grin that I wanted to peel off her face. Instead, I shoved my hand against the glass window and let my lone middle finger rise up like a new voice.

Our front walkway had turned slick and dangerous and I almost fell flat on my face like I had in fifth grade when Billy Montgomery plowed into me on a field trip and I had to get a root canal on my front tooth.

Once inside, my fear of being alone returned like a fast growing rash. I locked all the doors. I just knew that someone was watching me from outside, some crazy man who'd break into the house and grab me in the middle of the night. I couldn't believe that Blaire had left me.

The phone rang, which sent my mind into a flurry of worries. *It's the police. It's the hospital. The Mustang crashed. Mom got hit by a car.* I ran to it and, in my hurry, nearly dropped the receiver on the floor.

"Hello?" My heart pounded in my ears.

"Has she called yet?" It was Allie.

"No."

"They've probably lost track of time. You know, talking and whatever else."

"Yeah." I glanced at the clock. 4:30.

"They're probably making out. Sharon and her boyfriend make out for hours."

Maybe she was right. Maybe Danny and Blaire were rolling around in the snow, kissing like that scene in "Love Story" with the music soaring in the background.

"Call me the second she gets home," Allie said. "Okay?"

So if Blaire didn't come home tonight, she'd be back tomorrow. She'd waltz in that door, red-cheeked and freezing from the ride but relieved that Danny had come to his senses. The next day Mom would be home and she'd never have to know anything about Blaire's trip.

I made toast with peanut butter, poured a big glass of milk and brought both upstairs. If anyone broke in, I'd hear them sneak up the stairs and I'd be waiting behind the door with the glass, ready to smash it over the guy's head.

The phone rang. Probably Allie again. I ran into the hall.

"It's me." I could hear that long distance sound and I figured it was Mom calling from Chicago although I didn't really think two hours away qualified as long distance.

"Guess what?"

I was wrong. It was Sarah from Maryland.

"How'd you get my number?" I said.

"Guess who was found?"

My stomach fluttered. Like careful footsteps into a dark room, I asked, "The Hanley sisters?"

"Yup."

Do not believe her. It's another lie.

"I swear on a stack of bibles."

I bowed my head and squinted down at my sneakers. "You absolutely swear?"

"I absolutely swear."

I grabbed the words and seared them into my brain. If Robin were with me, she would've made the sign of the cross against her chest and said, "Praise the Lord!" in a fake southern accent.

"But wait," I said. "Are they okay?" I thought of the blonde pictures we'd seen on the news that spring day in our Maryland kitchen when Blaire had said, "I bet they're dead."

"They're fine. I mean, I guess."

I was scowling so hard that my forehead started to hurt. "So what happened? Who found them?"

"Some lady. In Montana."

"Mon*tana*?" My mind reeled.

"They were at some diner with this lady, and some guy who was sitting near them had a sister or something who lived in Maryland, so he knew all about the case."

"Wait," I said. "Didn't their mom live there?"

"Bingo."

I swallowed. "It was *her*? She *took* them?"

"Yup. She was the kidnapper."

My brain felt clogged.

"I guess it was a bad divorce or something. That's what my mom said. Something about custody."

"So she just *takes* them and doesn't tell anyone?"

"The news guy said the mom lives way out in the boondocks. She doesn't even have a phone. And get this: they didn't go to school 'cause she taught them at home. Weird."

"I don't get that."

"I know. So anyway, the lady at the diner called the police and all that and they came and it was this huge thing with a SWAT team and everything. It sounded kinda cool."

I sat on my bed. "I can't believe this."

"Aren't you happy? I thought you'd be bouncing off the walls."

"No, I am." Maybe it just wasn't sinking in yet. Or maybe part of me wouldn't let myself believe anything that she said. But the more I thought about it, the more I thought, *It's a sign.* The Hanley girls were safe and Blaire too would be safe. She and Mom would both return home and I wouldn't be alone anymore.

"I know you think I'm a liar and all that," she said.

I swallowed. "Are you lying about this?"

"I'm not. I swear. Ask anyone. The girls are safe at home."

I glanced out the window. The sky had turned grayish-white, the way it looks before it snows. "Did you see a picture of the mom?"

"Uh huh. She looked like a regular mom."

I wanted the kidnapper to be a total scuzz ball, not a person you were actually related to. Not your mom.

"They really were found?"

"Promise. They're safe at home. They're probably eating pizza right now."

"Or getting their ears pierced."

"What?"

I shook my head. "Nothing."

The girls were safe. They were alive. A giddiness rose up and I wanted to leap through the air. Blaire would be fine. People drove in the snow all the time. Everything would work out.

"Back to the lying thing," she said.

"What about it?"

"I swear on the Holy Bible that I'm not lying about this."

"What are you talking about?"

"The thing I told you before? About your dad? I have proof."

Before I had time to protest, she said, "The real estate lady told my mom that he shot himself in the basement and that's why your mom wallpapered it."

A chill started at the very tip of my head and coursed through my body and I wondered if that was what it felt like to be struck by lightning.

"The blood seeped into the concrete walls and they couldn't get it out," she said.

"Stop it! God! What's wrong with you?"

"Someone's not telling you the truth."

"It didn't happen!" I slammed down the phone.

Dad loved us. I knew that. It *had* to have been a mistake. It didn't make sense. People with major problems killed themselves. That wasn't Dad. And the word *gun* belonged to cop shows like "Baretta" and "The Streets of San Francisco"—not to our house and not to our dad.

But the wallpaper. I kept getting stuck on that. And people whispering at the funeral. The cremation. But why would Mom lie? That part made no sense.

Allie called again at 6:15.

"There's no way that happened," she said after I told her. "Your mom swore to you, right?"

"I know, but..." The hall light flickered, which sent my heart into over-drive. That was all I needed: the lights to go out.

"You think she's lying?" Allie said.

"No, I mean, why would she lie about something like that? She doesn't lie about stuff." But then I thought of Mom saying, "I decided that I have to pretend that he's on a trip." That was lying, right? To herself, but still.

The hall carpet beneath my feet was stained with little dribbles of dark brown—hot chocolate, maybe. I'd stood in the very same spot a hundred times and had never noticed them until now.

"She wallpapered the very next day," I said. "That's the weird thing."

"Yeah, but people wallpaper all the time."

"The day after your husband dies? Isn't that a weird time to do it?" My grip was tight around the receiver and I told myself to stop being so tense. To calm down and everything would be fine.

"Maybe she needed to keep busy, you know? Like keep her hands busy or something."

That was exactly what Mom had said. She'd needed a task, anything to focus.

"I dunno," I said, pulling the phone cord into Blaire's room and scan-ning her unmade bed and scattered clothes for answers. I turned to the dark lake, remembering how hopeful Mom had seemed when we first arrived in June, and me thinking, *This might actually be a good move. Things might be okay.* But now a strange girl was trying to convince me that my dad had killed himself in our house and, although I'd denied it on the phone, I wasn't so sure that it *wasn't* true. Was she the liar or was Mom?

"Look," Allie said, and I could just see her sitting on her bed, her legs folded underneath each other's, her knobby knees jutting out. I wanted to be eating Twinkies with her and talking about stupid things. Not this.

"You're the one who knows your dad," she said. "You'd know if he was going off the deep end, wouldn't you? I mean, that doesn't just come out of thin air, does it? Don't people have to be depressed or something?"

"Yeah, I think." I left Blaire's room and returned to my spot in the hallway.

"So was he?" she said.

"Depressed?" I squinted up at the ceiling, trying to make out the corners and hidden spaces of our house, places I'd never noticed, but everything seemed darker than ever.

"I'm up," she said. "I need to go."

"What? Where are you?"

"Locker room. I'm racing in five minutes."

"Oh." A pang seized me. I didn't want her to hang up.

"It's all gonna work out," she told me. "Just, you know... like, watch T.V. or something. Watch something funny. Or think about... I don't know. Think about Tommy."

If only I could stare out the window and daydream about Tommy instead of wondering if Dad had made the decision to leave us. When I thought, *No,* my mind kept going back to the basement.

I had to put it out of my mind. I had to. I couldn't be alone in the house and think that Dad had actually done that. Sarah was a liar. And Blaire was right: I needed to stop believing everything I heard.

After hanging up, I realized I hadn't even told her about the Hanley girls.

I tried to do homework, but I couldn't bear the silence. Each time a tree branch scratched against my window, a shot of adrenaline rushed through my veins. I went to Mom's dark room, unplugged the small T.V. and carried it to my room, setting it on top of the Merck Manual.

"Happy Days" was interrupted by a newsperson standing in front of a weather map, saying that residents in the Milwaukee area needed to brace for a winter storm, with gusts of wind up to forty miles an hour and two feet of snow falling by dawn. Great. Now Blaire would never get home. She'd skid, slide—whatever. She didn't know how to drive in the snow! Weren't there certain things you needed to know, like, When the car slid, you weren't supposed to step on the brakes? Or something? What about when your car flew into a ditch and you were buried alive?

Facts. That's what I needed to do. I grabbed my Math notebook, turned to a clean page and wrote every single Wisconsin fact I knew. *Famous Wisconsinites include Harry Houdini, Douglas MacArthur, Frank Lloyd Wright and...* I couldn't remember. *Wisconsin is known as the Beer Capital of the United States. The Ringling Brothers put on their first circus performance in...*

I tore out the page, crumpled it in a ball and flung it across the room, but it was like a poorly packed snowball and only traveled a few feet before plunging to the carpet.

Was it true? Mom would've told us, wouldn't she've? She had no reason to lie.

I drifted off at about two in the morning and woke at ten, thinking about the booklet in Mom's files, the one about cars made by Ford. Maybe it would say something about the Mustang tires being great in the snow. It was such a long shot. And I still wouldn't know if she'd actually arrived at Purdue or not. What I really needed to know—Was she alive or dead in a ditch?—wouldn't come from a quick search in Mom's drawer.

But still I went straight to her desk. That huge blue folder was in the same place as the last time. I took it out and brought it to my lap. Carefully I flipped through each section. Health insurance. Bank statements. I started to lose track of what I was looking for. It wasn't anything in particular—just something to make me go, *Ohhhhh. Right.* Something to knock the doubt out of my head that kept receding like a wave, then rushing forward again when I least expected it.

Ah *ha*. Ford Cars. 1966 Mustang. Perfect. I pulled it out and thumbed through it, searching for an answer.

An envelope fluttered to the carpet. It must've been inside the booklet. I picked it up. It wasn't the kind of envelope that had gone through the mail and had all the stamps. This only had two letters on it: DC. In capital letters. Washington, D.C., I figured. Maybe something about the sale of our Maryland house? Dad's job?

I unfolded it. It was more of a form. *Certificate of Death* the top said.

In the "name" box was his name. The date of his death was correct. A smaller box said "Cause of Death" and I read two words that Mom hadn't ever mentioned. Over and over, she'd said, "heart attack." But the death certificate said "cerebral hemorrhage." I scanned down to the bottom where, in an even smaller box, it said, "Self-inflicted."

My eyes blurred. I read it again. "Cerebral" meant brain, basically, and "hemorrhage" meant bleeding that didn't stop, so: brain bleeding. Bleeding brain. And "self-inflicted" meant he did it himself. He killed himself. But maybe it was a different Steven Wheeler and Mom just happened to have found a death certificate with his name on it and she kept it because she was weird. That would be like her. Sort of. Actually, not at all.

Self-inflicted. The words sat there, heavy as lead. *He died* was one thing, but *He killed himself* was a whole different story. A dark, secretive story that Mom could no longer deny.

Chapter 22

THE MORNING COLD slapped my face and stung my cheeks. I dragged myself all the way down the street and up the unshoveled hill. When I reached the top, gusts of wind whipped my cheeks. The words "self-inflicted" screeched through my brain like a reckless car.

I needed to tell someone. I needed to tell Blaire. But what if she got so upset that she killed herself? Was that what Mom meant when she talked about her being impulsive? Was suicide genetic?

A clap of thunder made my shoulders jump. The clouds broke like eggs, and rain poured all over me. Freezing rain. Sideways rain. Crazy Wisconsin winter rain. It blinded me.

I started to run, but the sidewalk was slick and I slipped and almost fell. I wanted to fall. I wanted physical pain to consume me.

More than once, Mom had looked straight in my eyes and said, "No, Martie. He had a heart attack." That and "End of story." I'd believed her. There was no reason for me not to.

It took about thirty minutes to get to Allie's. The railing outside of her house was wrapped in tiny yellow lights that twinkled in the rain. I walked up the brick steps to her front door and pushed the buzzer, but my fingertips were so numb that I couldn't tell if I'd actually pushed it. I scrunched my fingers together and pushed with my clenched fist until the door swung open. It was Tommy, wearing navy sweatpants and a white t-shirt, holding a yellow Nerf ball.

"Hey Martie, what's up?" He tossed the ball and caught it. I could feel the warmth coming from inside their house. Were cookies baking? Something smelled good, like warm cinnamon. Maybe oatmeal.

"Is Allie here?" I was out of breath.

"Allie!" he yelled up the stairs. Then he turned back to me. "I think she already left for practice. You okay?"

I nodded. My nose flared. I tried to stop my lips from trembling by biting them, but that only made my eyes water. Everything bubbled under the surface of my skin, like with one prick of a needle, everything would spurt out of me just as Blaire had predicted.

"Allie!" he yelled again, then shrugged. "They must've already left. Wait...lemme..." He ran to the kitchen and came back saying, "Yup. The keys are gone."

"Okay," I said, backing away. In our house we didn't have a reliable system like a key hook. You couldn't glance at it and know if a person was home or not. Blaire kept the Mustang key in her bedroom and Mom's keys always seemed to be lost at the bottom of her purse.

"You need something?" he asked.

"Like what?"

There were no secrets in their house, I just knew it.

"Like a ride home?"

"Ahmmmm..." I couldn't walk home. I'd get hypothermia and die of a heart attack.

"Okay," I said.

"Cool. Lemme grab my boots." He tossed the Nerf ball on the floor and came outside wearing a red down jacket and a black knit hat.

After we got on Lake Drive, he said, "So you were just...taking a walk in the snow and freezing rain?" He flashed a smile and, even though I'd just learned the most horrifying news of my life, I thought, I love him. I love Tommy.

"I needed to get out of the house," I said.

Along the curbs the snow had turned dark. It never stayed completely white, that was the problem with snow. It got dirty so fast that pretty soon you forgot all about how pretty it once was.

"How's Blaire?"

I turned to the windshield. "She's fine." Maybe Allie told him that she'd left.

"So she doesn't play tennis anymore?"

"I think my dad killed himself."

He braked and the car went sideways on the ice, nearly hitting the curb. "Jesus," he said.

I had no idea why I said, "I think." The truth was right there on paper.

He flipped on his blinker. I focused on the *tcktcktck* until he turned down our street and the steering wheel straightened out and the sound stopped.

"Are you serious?" He kept his eyes on the road, but I had a feeling that if he weren't driving, he'd be like Allie and go, "Oh my *Gahd*. What happened?"

"Does Allie know?"

I nodded and pointed to our house, which looked small with all the snow piled up, like it was trying to hide itself, except that it blazed with lights. "This is it."

Tommy put the car in Park and turned to me. He had Allie's eyes—brown and perfectly oval with that ring around the pupil. Just an hour ago, I'd held the death certificate in my hand, but now a tiny sliver inside me whispered, *But maybe it isn't true.*

"Are you okay?" he asked. "You want me to do anything?"

"Like what?"

He glanced at our house. "I don't know. I'm just really sorry. I feel bad for you."

I nodded, my fingers drumming against my cords, trying to count the hours Blaire had been gone, but I'd lost track.

"Okay, I should go," I said, shifting in my seat to face him.

"Sure you're okay?"

I nodded. I loved the way he looked at me, held every piece of me in his eyes. I could trust him. Tommy would never lie to me. Ever.

"Want me to walk you in?" he said.

I didn't know what got into me, but I lunged toward him and kissed him on the mouth like I knew exactly what I was doing. I'd kissed exactly one person in my life and that was as quick as a blink. But I was doing okay. Tommy kissed me back even though I was pretty sure that he had a crush on

Shelly Stires. Maybe he was pretending that I was her. I didn't care. Nothing mattered. His tongue, his lips, his hard chest. I wanted to disappear inside the kiss and never come out. We remained, lip-locked, until Julie's car drove in and parked right behind us. I pulled away from Tommy and peered into the side mirror.

"Who's that?" he said.

The passenger door opened and out stepped Mom in a new pair of brown boots that went up to her knees. Instead of a calm washing over me, everything inside me pulsed.

"I better go," I said to him, my gloved hand on the door handle. "I'm sorry I...you know...."

"Don't be." His eyes squinted like the sun had come out, and I kissed him again, hard.

I pushed open the car door and headed toward our house. From the corner of my eye, I saw Julie get out of the car and go to the trunk, her long hair floating in the wind.

I hurried over the icy path and reached for the door.

In back of me, Mom called, "Honey!"

I turned to her. A blue and yellow shopping bag dangled from her wrist. Her cheeks were red.

"Martie!" Julie called, waving. "Come say hi!"

I let myself in the house, kicked off my boots, then bolted up the stairs. I flung my soaked coat and hat and gloves in the bathtub. My clothes stuck to my skin and I peeled them off, changing into dry warm pants, turtleneck and a sweater. My arms and legs were cold and clammy and my clothes didn't slide over me the way I wanted them to.

When I shoved my frozen feet into itchy wool socks, I heard, "Whoo! It's cold!" Maybe when she came upstairs, I'd notice something in her expression that would explain why she lied. Maybe in the way she'd set down her suitcase or plop on her bed, I'd go, *Oh. Exactly. Now I see why she never told us.* I was waiting for magic.

"Martie!" I heard her boots rushing up the stairs. "Where did you go?"

I met her in the hallway, my hands clenched. I felt like an animal, ready to pounce.

"Who was driving that car?" she said. She smelled soapy, not at all like her normal self.

"Do I know that boy?" she said. "He looks older."

I just stared at her.

She frowned at me. "What's the matter? You're very pale." A wave of suspicion washed over her face. "Is everything alright? Where's Blaire?"

I had to tell Mom what I'd found, but part of me hesitated, like, *Maybe if I don't say anything, it'll go away*, but things didn't go away. They got worse.

"Martie! What happened?"

"I found the death certificate." A heavy bird flew out of my chest. I stared at her, waiting for her defense.

She didn't take my shoulders and say, "Martie, look at me. Your father had a heart attack." She didn't say, "End of story" or anything final like that. She said nothing and that was when I knew for sure that it was true. My dad had killed himself. Sarah had told me twice and I'd read the death certificate, but having Mom not deny it was the worst of all.

"Right?" I said. *Please say no please say no. Please. Say. No.*

What she did instead of answering directly was come toward me with her arms out the way Aunt Julie did, tilting her head like, *Oh, poor Martie*.

I stepped away. I didn't want her sympathy.

"I know this is a shock for you," she said, eying me like I was a wild animal, capable of ripping her to shreds.

"You said he had a heart attack! I asked you specifically!"

"I know." She looked down.

"You lied to me!" My words flung straight at her face and she winced, her eyes filling with tears. "How could you do that?"

"I couldn't bear it," she said. "I just couldn't. To tell you that your own father has—"

"But it's Dad!" I wanted to shake her. "That's why you did the wallpaper, right?"

"I had to do *some*thing. I couldn't just—"

"You said you did it because you needed to do something with your hands. I *knew* that seemed weird! Why did I ever believe you? God!"

"Come in my room," she said. "Please."

I should've refused, but I felt like she might lead me to another piece of important information, though what more could there be?

She put down her suitcase and sat on her bed. "Come," she said, patting it twice.

I didn't move an inch.

She breathed in deeply and said, "He'd been hospitalized."

"You mean the virus?"

She looked at me straight-on. "There was no virus."

I squinted. "What?"

"He had a nervous breakdown, Martie. That's why he'd been in the hospital."

My mind went blank like Mom had yanked a cord out of the wall and everything went dead. Crazy people in movies had breakdowns. People who tore out their hair and talked to themselves in public. I didn't want to know those people. And now Mom was telling me that Dad was one of them.

"It happens sometimes," she said.

My heart pounded. A fog sailed into both ears and, for a second, I only heard scraps of what she said.

"...got depressed... overwhelmed... couldn't function."

I focused on her mouth, which had closed now, forming a straight line like the horizon. How many more lies were behind it?

"He couldn't get out of bed," she said. "Everything overwhelmed him. Everything, Martie. You can't imagine."

"Why didn't we know this?"

She turned away. "I promised him I wouldn't tell you. He was... embarrassed."

My fingers pressed on my temples, something I'd seen people do in movies when they had throbbing headaches. "But if he went to the hospital," I said, trying to grab at loose pieces. "Didn't that help?"

"Yes, but..." she sighed. "He got depressed again."

I remembered how thin and serious Dad had seemed when he returned from the hospital. Blaire had raced outside to hug him while I stayed at the window, thinking, *Something's different* but telling myself that the virus must've made him tired.

"Suicide is…" Mom shook her head. "It's a terrible, terrible thing. And you're left with all these questions. Questions that have no answers."

I stood on burning coals, switching from one foot to another, from Mom's lie to Dad's suicide.

"I don't get it," I said, her words spinning inside me. "If he got depressed again, then why didn't he go back to the hospital?"

She got up from the bed. "He thought he could handle it. He thought quitting his job was the answer, but…"

How could I've been so out of it? Yes, I knew he quit his job, but I thought it was because he wanted to focus more on his painting.

"I don't *get* this!" I screamed. "So why did he *kill* himself? Normal people don't do that!"

"They do," she said, walking to her dresser. "Some people do. If they're out of sorts like he was."

Out of sorts. I hated those words.

She unzipped her boots and stepped out of them. "Don't you remember all those weeks he stayed in bed?"

"He was sick!"

"He was depressed. And unstable." She removed her earrings. "And he spent all of our money."

"All of it?"

"That was the impulsive side of him. He'd get an idea and that was it. There was never any process."

"But he was fun," I said, trying to grab onto something solid.

"Yes," she said. She unfastened the pearls from around her neck, and when she took them off, the string broke and pearls dropped all over her white carpet like hail.

"Oh for God's sake." She fell to her knees, her fingers raking them up.

"I don't get this whole thing." It was all I could say.

She stood and poured the broken necklace into her top drawer where she kept underwear and bras and other things that she wore close to her skin, and I thought of all the times she lied to me wearing all those things. Panty hose and slips and sleeveless shirts with skirts. Nightgowns. She lied in every single room. With makeup and without. Wet hair, dry hair. One huge lie repeated over and over.

I left the room. The walk took forever. I noticed every spec in the carpet, each particle in the air.

I sat at my desk without moving. I opened my notebook to a new page. I held the pen so tightly that the tip of my index finger turned white. Instead of writing, I dug my pen tip into the paper and pressed down hard, shimmying it from side to side, trying to break through the whole notebook.

Finally I knew the truth, the one I'd been searching for all this time. Why wasn't I relieved?

The phone rang twice. Mom must've picked up. Maybe it was Sarah calling back to say, "Just kidding!" I didn't want to ever answer the phone again.

"Martie!" Mom yelled. Her new boots shuffled against the hallway carpet. "We need to get Blaire!"

My pulse rushed. "Is she okay?"

"The car broke down. She's at a gas station. Get your coat."

The blanket that Mom had tried to secretly throw out sat in a heap at the foot of my bed. I grabbed it for Blaire. Or maybe it was for me.

Chapter 23

"BLAIRE PICKING UP and leaving like that is exactly the kind of behavior that worries me," Mom said in the car after ten minutes of silence.

I tried to make out the highway in front of us through the snow that blew across the windshield. "She needed to see Danny."

"Well, she didn't need to drive into a snow storm by herself in that car." Mom's shoulders were hunched as she leaned into the wheel. "Thank God she's all right."

"Were you ever planning on telling us?"

"Martie, please look for the exits. I don't want to miss the turn. This is very difficult driving in all this snow."

"You were never gonna tell us, were you?"

"Is that it?" she pointed. "Does that say Exit 23?"

We pulled into the Texaco station where the Mustang sat, caked in snow. The wind blew so hard that the gas sign rattled and I worried it might break loose and fly into us.

I squinted and saw a man inside the station wearing a dark ski jacket and hat. He sipped from a Styrofoam cup.

"Where is she?" I said.

Mom put the car in Park. "Wait here." She pushed open her door. As she rushed toward the station, her hair flew wildly in the wind. It reminded me of Tricia Nixon's blonde hair whipping in her face as she and her family made their way to the helicopter after the President's farewell speech.

All I could think was, *I need to tell Blaire, I need to tell Blaire,* but when I saw the two of them walking to the car, holding onto each other, I thought, *It'll crush her.* I couldn't do it. Not now.

I ran out into the freezing air that smelled of gasoline and nighttime. All of my worry from the past two days surged through me until it broke open and burst like a fire hose. I flung my arms around her, burying my face in her shoulder, which wasn't really shoulder but hard cold fabric. I couldn't remember the last time we'd hugged—why didn't we hug more often? She seemed cold and thin, an armful of bones. I wanted to pick her up and carry her to the warm car.

"Something happened," I blurted out. I needed her to feel as cheated and betrayed as I did. "Something you're not gonna believe."

"I can't," she said, shaking her head. "Not now."

Did she know what I was about to say? No. She couldn't have. Maybe she thought I was about to tell her something stupid, like how I finally spoke up to Mom. Or that I'd kissed Tommy.

Seconds later the three of us were safe inside the car with the engine idling and the heat blasting. Blaire was in back, huddled under the blanket.

Mom pulled out of the station and we headed into the blur of white while the wipers swung frantically across the glass.

"It looks like it's getting worse out there," I said, but I guess Mom didn't hear me or else she was just focused on getting us onto the highway and not plowing into the car in front of her.

⟶⟵ ⟶⟵

My legs were heavy as I climbed the stairs to the second floor, my head pounding with each step. All I wanted was to be sound asleep, far away from the truth. Either that or making out with Tommy in the front seat of his car, oblivious to anything except our shared breath. I pulled on sweat pants and a big t-shirt and slid under the cool sheets, my shoulders beginning to twitch as I gradually felt my body starting to drift away.

A knock on the door jumpstarted my heart.

"Martie?"

Mom's voice.

Go away go away go away.

She pushed open the door and came into my dark room and sat on my bed. I could hear her breathing and the sound of her lips parting as she opened her mouth, clearly about to say something, then hesitating and starting over.

"I know you're confused and angry right now," she said. "You have every right to be."

I clenched my fists, trying to find warmth deep in my palms.

"It's a lot to digest, and I guess…well, I guess that's why I kept it from you. I didn't want you to have to go through this."

"He was my father!" I yelled.

Her eyes closed. "I know. But as a parent—"

I pulled the blanket over my head.

"Martie, please let me—"

Go! my whole body screamed. *Get out of my room!* She must've received the message; she got up and left, but not without putting her hand on what she thought was—what?—my head? shoulder?—actually it was the inside of my elbow—and telling me she loved me. I didn't care. I didn't love her.

I waited until she was down the hall to open my bedside drawer and take out the folded death certificate. How many other important things had I not figured out? I turned on the light and read every single word. *Self-inflicted.* I read it over and over until the words bled into each other and separated and finally turned dark and I dropped off to sleep.

In the morning I woke to a wet spot on my pillow where I must've been drooling. I squinted at the calendar that hung on the back of my door. Sunday. The clock said 11:30. The truth hung in the air, prodding me, pulling me out of bed and pushing me into Blaire's room where she stood on a chair, pulling out thumbtack after thumbtack. Pictures fell to the floor—Danny holding a basketball, Danny pushing Blaire in a pool, Danny's face behind sunglasses.

"I have to tell you something," I said, the words like a speeding train. "Something major."

A picture of Blaire with her blonde streak fell onto her pillow. She untacked more and more and they dropped to the carpet. Three, four, five, ten of them, landing on top of each other. Twenty, thirty pictures from when Blaire had long hair.

"Danny and I broke up," she said. "I can't handle anything else right now. Can you just..."

"It's about Dad." I couldn't stop. "It's horrible. It's...the worst thing you could imagine."

She stepped off the bed, her bare feet landing on the pictures. "What?"

"He..." Just three words, but I couldn't say one of them. I glanced out the window, then gazed right into her eyes. "He didn't have a heart attack."

"What are you talking about?"

"He didn't. I know he didn't." The folded death certificate was tight in my hand. Evidence.

"So what happened then?"

I couldn't. Or didn't want to. "Mom lied to us."

"About what?"

"He killed himself," I whispered, the words dripping with slime.

"Who told you that?"

"Mom. And the girl in Maryland who lives in our house. She said that the real estate person told her."

She squinted. "Wait. *What?* Mom told you that?"

"I found the death certificate. *And* she told me. It was...it says it. It says *cerebral hemorrhage.*" I presented it like a gift, but she didn't take it. "She's been lying this entire time." My heart raced, waiting for her to be as outraged as I.

Her eyes closed like a window shade going down and I thought, Oh God. I shouldn't have told her. She was too emotional. She and Danny had just broken up and now she was finding out the truth about Dad. She wouldn't be able to take it. I was the resilient one, after all.

"I'm sorry," I said. "I shouldn't've…"

"I knew," she said, her eyes a cool shade of blue.

"What?"

"I knew he killed himself. I knew the whole time."

My head leaned forward. "*What?*"

I stared at her mouth and it looked smaller than normal, pinched, the way Mom's looked when she wore too much dark lipstick.

"She made me lie."

"*Mom* did?" The words spun in a thousand directions. I put my fingers to my temples. "Wait. You *knew*…that he killed himself? That Dad—"

"I found him, Martie. I found him laying there in the basement."

My heart bashed inside my chest and a coldness washed over me like a bucket of ice freezing me to the core. "You didn't *tell* me?"

A ragged lock of hair near her left ear stuck out and I wanted to grab it and pull it out of her scalp. She looked like a boy. Someone I didn't know.

"Martie," she said.

I covered my ears. I took the stairs by twos, grabbed my coat, stepped into my boots and ran out back into the bitter cold. Pieces of me broke apart and fell on top of the lawn, which wasn't lawn anymore but weeks and weeks of winter layered on top of each other. When I got to the end of the yard, I jumped down to the beach. I wanted to fall like a five-year-old in a padded snowsuit and not be hurt. Instead, I landed hard on my hands and knees and stayed there, the lump in my throat bursting out of my mouth. Thin strands of saliva dripped from my lips like icicles. Dad killed himself. Dad shot himself in the head.

"Martie!" Blaire yelled, running toward me. I didn't want to talk to her. Her and Mom. Liars. They'd shared their secret and lied to me. And all that time I'd thought Mom and I were paired together. What an idiot I was. I had no one.

I got up and walked onto the frozen lake. Surrounding me for as far as I could see was hardened snow that swooped up into drifts, like frozen waves that a person could disappear behind without anyone knowing.

"Wait!" she called.

Maybe I was the impulsive one because all I wanted to do was keep going until I couldn't go any further. I didn't want to die; I just wanted to not feel anything.

"Martie, *wait.*"

The further I went, the windier it got. My cheeks stung. The inside of my nose burned. I wanted to run for the unfrozen water and jump in so that everything would be finished. Blank. Was that how Dad felt?

"Just *wait.* Stop for a minute."

I swung around. "What?"

She stood there in her down coat, crying. Why was *she* crying? She wasn't the one who'd been lied to all that time.

"I *wanted* to tell you," she said, coming closer but still keeping her distance. "You have no idea how hard it was keeping it from you."

"Then why did you do it? You never even listen to Mom! Why did you listen to her about that?"

"Because...it was horrible. And you were young. I couldn't imagine you knowing. It would've messed you up."

"Don't you think I'd want to know? God! What's wrong with you?"

I kicked a pile of snow, but it was solid ice and killed my foot. I wanted to keep kicking until every part of me was numb.

A rumbling started underneath my boots, followed by a series of cracks. I'd read something about cracking sounds on the ice, but now I'd forgotten if it was a normal sound or a warning sign. Maybe it meant the ice was breaking apart in chunks, floating away in different directions. Maybe I'd stand on a piece and let it take me to Illinois, where I could stand on that building and see four states at once.

"Come inside," she said.

"No."

"Martie, come on. You'll get frostbite."

After a few more minutes, the wind picked up. I wanted to stay out in the cold and never go back inside—no, I wanted to leave Mom and Blaire. Leave the house and everything in it and go live with people who told me the truth because they knew I needed to hear it. But the air was so sharp that it cut my skin. I turned and headed back to the house, defeated.

.

Chapter 24

I SPENT THE rest of the day in my room. They both knocked on my door, begging to talk to me, but I didn't let them in. I didn't want to do one thing for either of them.

When it got dark, Mom told me through the door that she'd ordered a pizza. When I didn't answer, she said, "You need to eat," and for the first time ever, the alarm in her voice wasn't directed at Blaire.

I thought of how different I might be if all along I'd known the truth. Would it have scarred me more than learning that my family had lied to me? I doubted it. If I'd known, I wouldn't have been distracted all year and full of doubt and wondering if I was crazy for doubting. My heart racing. My body knowing that something wasn't right.

I got up and went to my desk to grab my notebook, the one I'd abandoned after Dad had died. There was no entry saying that he'd had a heart attack or had passed away or any of that. Just blank on the day he died. And blank every page after that. I remembered thinking that if I didn't write it, then maybe it wouldn't be true.

Someone knocked on my door.

"I know you don't want to talk," Blaire said, barging in, wearing faded Levis and a plaid flannel shirt, "but for like four months Danny's had another girlfriend. He never told me that. I had to catch him in a lie."

"And?" I stared at her, too impatient to listen to her breakup story.

"And I just stood there, like, How could I not have known this?"

I wanted to slap her. "You think Danny cheating on you is the same as you and Mom lying to me?" My heart pounded. I still couldn't completely make sense of it all.

"I know it's not the same, but—"

"Every time I brought it up, you said, 'No, Martie. It was a heart at-tack.' And 'Why can't you just accept that he died?' God!" There was no stopping me now. I'd pushed the resilient Martie off the boat and now a new angry version of myself had taken the helm.

My mind went back to all those times when Mom and Julie sat in the living room, talking in hushed voices, quiet as mice. Maybe all along Julie had been telling her to stop lying to me.

"Are you done?" I said.

"Martie, please." She reached for me, but I jerked away.

"Don't do this," she said. "Don't shut me out."

I squinted at her. "'Don't shut me out'? Are you serious? What do you think you and Mom did for an entire year?"

"I know and I'm sorry. We both are."

My eyes closed. "Go. Please."

We. All along they'd been a team.

After she left, I pressed my pen against the light blue lines.

It was all a lie.

Words dribbled out like juice squeezed from a dry lemon.

I filled two lines, but it didn't shrink the lead ball in my stomach or dis-solve the lump in my throat.

I wrote what Mom finally admitted and what Blaire knew all along. A layer peeled off, which I thought would feel like relief, but it felt like a bad sunburn that stung each time I moved.

Didn't it bother Dad that he'd never make homemade bread with us again? Did it cross his mind to say goodbye?

"Write about everything," Mrs. Neely had said in the beginning of the school year. "Especially the things that hurt."

⊷⊱⊰⊶

When I woke, a soft orange glowed on the lake. Fresh powder covered the lawn. Snow on top of snow on top of snow. I couldn't see how we'd ever get to spring.

I dressed in my warmest clothes and snow boots and went out the back door before anyone woke.

The snow crunched as I trudged through it. On top was new snow from the past day, which was slightly hard, like a sheet of crystals had formed on top. My boots plowed through the layers until I got to the edge of our yard where, like yesterday, I jumped the two feet instead of climbing down the ladder because I had no clue where the ladder hid under the snow.

The wind had formed snowdrifts, some taller than I. Like crude pyramids. I walked along the lake, parallel to the houses. I just wanted to keep moving. One foot in front of the other. The ice under my feet rumbled, the sound resembling a faraway engine. No one was around. I had the whole lake to myself. Blaire might've said, "Yeah, no one's that stupid to go out on the frozen lake," but I didn't care. What did I have to lose? I'd already lost Dad and now Blaire and Mom weren't lost to me, but they'd shoved me off the raft where we'd all been floating and now I flailed between waves, sinking with each breath.

Another rumble rose up, louder than the last one, letting off a series of cracks. I thought about Allie saying that weird things happened in the lake, how people disappeared. Dogs died in there. They'd chase a bird all the way out to the thin ice and fall right in the freezing water.

I headed to the snow-covered rocks along the shore. In the summer I'd gotten so good at jumping rock to rock, but the landscape was so different now. I had nothing to hold onto, no footing.

I picked up a handful of snow, packed it and threw it onto the ice where it splattered like a water balloon.

Why did I even call our old number in the first place? If I'd never talked to Sarah, then she never would've told me anything and if I didn't know anything, I wouldn't be feeling the way I did.

"It's a gorgeous mystery, no?" a voice to the right of me said.

A few feet away, the witch stood, wearing a big navy coat that looked like it might've belonged to a man. It went all the way down to her dark winter boots.

She walked toward me, her eyes squinting. "Martie," she said when she got close. "Right?"

I hadn't seen her up close since that day in the fall when Blaire pushed me up the bus aisle, desperate to meet her. If you could get past the wrinkles, her face exuded light. But still there was something hard in it that didn't seem to have anything to do with age.

"An enormous body of water," she said, squinting at the lake. "With so many secrets."

The brittle wind blew back the loose grey wisps around her face.

"Come," she said. "I'll show you my view."

I didn't even flinch. I followed her over snow-covered rocks, but the snow was so deep that I couldn't tell what was rock and what was the crevice between rocks. I fell twice—once on my side and once straight forward, landing on my elbows. The witch soldiered on, her long dark coat trailing against the snow like a cape. Maybe she was leading me to my death. I didn't care.

When we got to her beach, everything was frozen the way it was at our house, but ours seemed to have more snow drifts. At the witch's, you could see straight out to the dark water beyond the ice.

"Each day I come down and see what the waves have brought me," she said.

"My friend's brother once found a dog skeleton on the beach."

"Yes," she said. "The ice causes many unfortunate accidents."

"So what sort of things have you found?"

"Driftwood, glass, shells." She shrugged. "Boat sidings, bottles. You name it."

"What's the weirdest thing you've found?"

A smile lifted the corners of her mouth. "A large piece of porcelain that I later discovered was part of a toilet."

"How did a toilet…"

She kept her gaze on the water. "I've found parts of beautiful china dolls. Arms, legs. Some faces." She turned to me. "Care to see them?"

"Me?"

She smiled and winked. "I won't bite."

Maybe she was messing with me, like, *I know you think I'm a witch and I actually really am, so I'll act like I'm all jokey about it.*

Regardless, I went.

Inside painted faces stared at me. A line of clay figures sat on a windowsill. Round flat stones the size of pancakes were stacked on a side table. I thought of her saying, "I believe we can express ourselves through everything we come in contact with."

She reached for the doorknob to a closet.

Hesitant, I went toward her, my ski jacket swishing with each step.

Inside the closet were built-in sliding drawers. She pulled out the middle one. A graveyard of doll parts. Elbows, ears, painted lips, one rosy cheek, part of a pale pink foot. And full faces that stared up at me, wide-eyed with rosy pouts.

"All these were in the lake?"

She sat on a bench, unlaced her boots and pulled them off. On her feet were thick grey socks. "Over many years," she said. "Some were stuck between rocks or hidden under leaves." She rose. "But yes, the waves carried them in."

"My dad loved the water."

She removed her coat and hung it on a wooden hook. "I'm sorry you lost him."

"Thank you." It had been a long time since anyone—especially an adult—had said that.

Her gaze remained fixed on me until I turned away. "Do you live alone?"

"Mmhm." She took off her gloves and hat.

"It doesn't scare you?"

"Scare me?"

"You know, like people trying to...break in?"

"No, no. It doesn't scare me." She rubbed her hands together. "Besides, the only people who want to come to this house are drunk teenagers."

Allie had told me about older kids driving down to her house, daring each other to scale the fence and ring her doorbell.

"Once every few months I come down to a broken window and a beer bottle on my floor."

"Do you have kids?" It was a sudden off-the-topic question, but I needed to know if there was any truth behind the rumors.

"Sit down," she said, gesturing to a worn purple armchair next to the stone fireplace.

I sat and she did, too—across from me—in another chair. She fiddled with that pouch she wore around her neck. She unzipped it and took out what looked like a business card.

"Johnnie and Liam," she said, handing it to me.

A photo of two boys, brown-haired and tan, playing in the sand together, smiling easily.

"These are your kids?"

She displayed a second photo of a bearded man on a boat.

"My three loves." She half-smiled, looking down at the photos.

"Where are they now?" I said. "Are they..."

"They're gone."

I swallowed. "You mean..."

"I stared out that window for months," she said. "I was sure that one day they'd march right back in this house."

I wanted to reach over and touch her. Three family members, gone? All at once?

At first glance, after she'd handed me the photos, I'd seen two cute boys playing and a man on a boat, but now I saw a husband and father struggling in the deep, cold water, trying to reach his sons whose small arms disappeared under the surface.

"What did you do?" I asked. "I mean, how did you..."

"Terrible things happen in life," she said. "Great losses."

I realized why she kept her eyes on the lake—not that she expected her family to reappear after all those years, but just knowing they were out there—maybe it helped.

We didn't have an actual gravesite for Dad and I had no idea if or when we'd be back along the Chesapeake Bay—or even Rock Creek Park, for that matter.

"I'm so sorry," I said. "That's..." There were no words. I couldn't believe that people had turned her tragedy into something awful that *she'd* done.

"Yes," she said, turning away from the window, "but after a certain point...Well, you never forget. Ever. But you can't lie down and die yourself. No."

She stood and walked to the door, which I guess meant that our visit was over.

"I'll never have answers," she said as she put her hand on the knob. "I'll never know exactly what went wrong that day in the boat."

I couldn't imagine the number of hours she'd spent staring out at the dark lake, trying to picture the events of that day.

I stepped into the cold, bright morning where I'd been earlier, but the air felt warmer now. Or maybe the wind had died down.

Her yard looked so different covered in snow. And all the faces. Up close they weren't as scary. Twigs for eyebrows, stones for ears. A curved shell for a mouth. Each one was different yet they shared a surprised expression like a snapshot, frozen in time. Joy, interrupted.

I turned to her. She stood on the outside step, her wrinkly face to the sun.

"Why do you make all these faces?"

She tugged on her scarf the same way my dad loosened his tie after a day of work. "It was all I kept seeing," she said. "Every time I shut my eyes, they were there, the three of them. So close I could almost touch them."

I glanced at the huge face sprouting out of the snow.

"So I drew them," she said. "And painted them. And found pieces from the lake to construct them." She smiled, pleased.

"Your sister made one."

"Blaire? Really?"

"Right over here." She headed to the back of the house where a figure stood—tall logs in an upside down v for legs, no arms or torso—just a round slice for a head. Twigs were crow's feet. A gathering of acorns formed his eyes. And the mouth was made of fish scales, which must've taken forever. I had no idea how she'd attached everything to the face. Sap? Something from nature. Not glue.

"Isn't it wonderful?"

I nodded, thinking how strange and amazing it was that a figure of Dad now stood in the witch's yard.

"She said she wanted him to have the best view of the lake." The sun hit the witch's eyes and they gleamed like something magical was behind them.

"At times you think you won't make it, but you will."

I bit my lip. I wanted her to keep telling me that I'd be okay, over and over, until I'd feel it myself because I had no idea how I'd ever be okay about any of it.

"They lied to me," I said in a small voice.

"Yes," she said like she knew all about it.

"For almost an entire year."

"People make mistakes," she said.

They weren't just mistakes, though—they were lies. Lies on top of lies.

"If I'd known the truth," I said, "everything would be different."

"Would it?"

"Yes," I said, turning away. "Definitely."

I could tell she was trying to lock eyes, but I didn't want to face her. Just because her family died didn't mean that she knew everything.

⚊⧓⚊

At home the kettle screamed.

I kicked off my boots and stepped over the slivers of frozen snow that had fallen from the treads of my shoes and now lay against the wood floor like potato chip shards from the bottom of the bag.

"Martie, wait," Mom said, turning off the gas flame.

"I can't." I rushed toward the stairs and ran to my room where the horrible truth hung in the air.

I went to my bureau and pulled out the top drawer. Pushing my balled-up socks aside, I reached for the jar.

It was a sunny day when we poured part of his ashes in the Chesapeake. But the following week, when we stood on a bridge above Rock Creek, the wind blew in gusts and the ashes drifted in the air, aimless. We went down to the actual water to pour them in, which felt unimportant and too quick, like we were trying to get rid of a secret. We were. I just didn't know it then. Mom's rushed footsteps in the parking lot, the empty urn thrown against the passenger seat, and the two of us in the back, looking out our separate windows. Everything made sense now.

I returned the jar to its place in the drawer, then went downstairs and put my boots and coat back on.

From the kitchen, Mom called, "Where're you going now?"

I closed the front door behind me. I knew exactly where I was going.

Chapter 25

THE HEEL OF my boot slipped on the front walkway and I fell on my side, my shoulder slamming against the ice. "*Damn*it!" I yelled into the brittle air.

I limped to the garage, which was open. Of course the Mustang wasn't there. It was still at that gas station near exit 23. Danny. What a jerk. Totally cheating on her. Tommy would never do that.

My shoulder ached. And my side and hip. I scanned the few items hanging on hooks—a ladder, two shovels, a rake—but none of us had touched them since Dad had died. He was the raker, the shoveler, the guy who climbed the ladder to scoop wet leaves out of the gutter.

I couldn't keep thinking that way, though—that Dad made the turkey and Dad did everything. He was gone! And none of those things would happen anymore unless *we* did them. I'd have to figure out how to cook a not-frozen turkey that actually tasted good. And when I learned how to drive, maybe I'd be the one hopping in the front seat with my sunglasses, saying, "Let's get ice cream!"

I took the shovel off the wall and dragged it to the front walkway.

I dug it in the snow and tossed the load. I did it three more times and then realized I couldn't keep flinging the snow right near the walkway or else I'd have to shovel that whole pile, too, so I re-shoveled the snow and flung it a few yards away. Snow was a weird thing. I'd never thought before about having to put it somewhere. Plus it was heavy. One brutal winter when we drove downtown to see the lighting of the White House Christmas tree, I'd noticed mountains of dirty snow piled on street corners.

My dad had shrugged. "There's nowhere else to put it."

The front door opened and Mom came out, bundled in Dad's olive green wool coat that came down to her shins. It was bulky on her and made her look small, almost mousy.

"Can we talk?" she said.

I dug the sharp tip of the shovel into the snow again. "You and Blaire lied to me for an entire year."

"I know," she said in a voice so thin I barely heard her. "I thought I was protecting you. I didn't realize the harm I was causing." She stepped toward me. "I'm so sorry."

I could barely lift the mound. My lower back ached as I walked it over to the pile and dumped it. I couldn't get over the weight of it.

"When I was your age, I knew all about my mother's worries. I could recite every single reason why she hated my father." Mom shook her head like the memory was so close to her that she could grab it and squeeze it in her hand. "The last thing I wanted was for you to grow up, burdened, the way I was."

My skin felt prickly under my sweater. "Every time I asked you about it, you denied it."

"I know I did. And I regret that. I really do, Martie. I know I've let you down."

"You lied every single time."

She nodded, guilty. Her nose had turned pink from the cold.

Another shovel-ful. Dig, scoop, toss. "What about Julie? Was she in on it, too?"

"She thought it would be best if you knew the truth."

I looked up. "Then why didn't *she* tell me?"

"Because I'm your mother, that's why."

She stood there, a shivering figure lost in her dead husband's wool coat. I looked at the slope of her shoulders, remembering my little hands rubbing sunscreen into her warm skin.

"I know this is hard to understand now," Mom said. "But as a parent I had to shield you from it. Suicide is not something that kids should know about. It's an awful thing."

"Why did he *do* it then?"

Mom sighed and looked away. "That's something we may never know."

I hated that answer. How were we supposed to live with that?

"You know that it had nothing to do with any of us, right? He loved you. I know that. It's nothing you did or didn't do. This was a very deep issue within himself."

"But what *was* the issue?"

"I don't know exactly what it was, but he was depressed. Clinically depressed."

"Well he didn't have to *leave* us! God!" The shovel hit the walkway. The unmistakable *chht!* of metal scraping stone.

"I know. Believe me."

Sweat dribbled down my sides. A rage filled me. I wanted to yell at him, "How could you do this to us? You jerk!" I'd never been mad at him before now.

"To do something like that—to take your own life—that's..." She squinted into the cold air between us, trying to see something. "...he wasn't thinking in a rational way."

Blisters had formed on my palms and now it hurt to grasp the shovel the way I'd been doing.

"Do you believe me, Martie? That I wasn't intentionally trying to hurt you?"

But I wasn't finished with the last thing she'd said, and even more—I began to realize the reason that Blaire had been so mad at Mom for so long. She blamed her. "So if you knew he was depressed," I said. "Then why couldn't you do anything about it? Why did you let him...?"

Mom, in a different, harder tone, said, "Look at me, Martie."

My eyes, reluctant to meet hers, focused beyond her, at the front door where our wreath still hung, dropping dry needles each time we opened or closed the door.

"I loved your father," she said. "And I knew he was suffering, but..." She bit her bottom lip. "I had no idea he was capable of something like that. No idea whatsoever."

Small patches of ice remained on the stones, but mostly the path was clear.

"Was that really what he wanted?" I asked Mom. "To never see us again?"

"That was the last thing he wanted."

I thought of the time in Florida when a giant wave was about to crash on me, and Dad yelled, "Hold your breath!" Squeezing my eyes shut, I let the force of the ocean sweep my small body upside down until I disappeared inside the froth, my nose filling with water and my eyes burning from salt. And now I felt a similar kind of upside down, not knowing if or when I'd come up for air.

I tipped the shovel forward and watched it land on the mound of snow.

"He loved all of us," Mom said. "I know that with every bit of my heart."

She looked taller somehow, like now the coat fit her.

"Okay," I said. "I'm done."

And for the first time all winter, I walked up our front path without bracing myself for a fall.

⟵⟶

I couldn't sleep. Each time I closed my eyes, everything rushed by me like a slideshow—pictures of Mom and Dad on the beach; Dad at the grill, flipping chicken; Blaire pressing her lips together as she whacked a tennis ball across the net; Mom shimmying a "For Sale" sign into the dry earth. Dad riding the waves; Dad walking down to the basement. And me on the sidelines, trying to sort it all out.

At three-fifteen in the morning, I got up and went to Blaire's room. She was wide awake, wearing sweat pants and a baggy long-sleeved shirt. She sat on top of her covers, drawing in the sketchpad on her lap. I hadn't really looked at her since the day she took off in the Mustang, determined to make things right again with Danny. Mom had called Blaire impulsive, but there was no way that she shared Dad's type of impulse. Did she? How did a person know if he or she were, as Allie would say, going off the deep end?

"Hey," I said like it was a normal time to be awake.

She looked up, her eyes still squinting from concentrating. "You okay?" Her hair sprung this way and that. Not one piece lay flat against her scalp.

I nodded from habit, which I was starting to realize was a pretty bad habit—acting like I was always fine. "Actually, no," I said.

Her desk chair was piled with clothes, so I sat on the carpet. My legs felt heavy. My shoulders and back ached from shoveling. "The day it happened," I said. "Were you home?"

She inhaled deeply and held the breath a second before letting it out. From Mom she'd inherited the balloon breath and now I'd probably start doing it, too.

"I was at school," she started. "And I realized I'd forgotten my tennis shoes. It was like three o'clock and I had that match at four, so I ran home to get them. Only I couldn't find them anywhere."

Above Blaire's head was the wall that used to be Dannyland. Now it had become a white field of tiny dots where the thumbtacks had once been.

"Then I remembered that I'd stepped in dog crap the day before—remember? From that stupid Arlo?"

I nodded. I did remember. Blaire'd said, "Stupid dog!" and picked up a stick from the ground to remove the mess from the soles of her shoes, but it had already settled deep in the grooves. Later, when Mom had gotten home from work, she'd thrown them in the wash machine, saying, "Carol Specter's a lovely person, but that dog needs to go."

"And then what?" I said.

"So, yeah, I remembered they were downstairs and I was freaking out 'cause I realized they probably weren't even dry."

My eyes were fixed on Blaire's mouth. My fingers and toes curled, braced for the next word.

"So I started going down the cellar stairs. Like, one, two, maybe four steps, and I was looking straight at that wall ahead, you know? That concrete wall? Like if you walked down all the steps and kept going, you'd run into the wall, right?"

Of course I knew. Why was she going into such detail as if I hadn't gone up and down those steps a million times?

"There was this weird break in the wall," she said. "Not a break, but a crack."

"Uh huh."

"I looked at that, not thinking anything, just sort of going down the stairs, you know? Then I turned and…"

I sat, knees to my chest, hugging my legs. "And what?" I tried to picture the gory scene.

"And I guess I called the police. I don't remember."

"You don't re*mem*ber?" It felt like another lie.

Blaire's eyes narrowed. "I was in shock. It's not a normal thing, Martie—finding your dad like that."

I nodded and looked down. "Sorry."

She grabbed her sketchbook and tossed it to me.

"What's this?"

"Just look."

I opened it, flipping through the images. For about thirty pages or so, she'd drawn almost the exact same thing, each one a slightly different version of a lightning bolt. Page after page.

"I couldn't get it out of my head," she said. "The crack in the wall. That crooked shape was all I could see."

The witch had said the exact same thing about her family's faces. Faces that haunted her until she turned them into art.

"It was the last thing I saw before everything changed. The last bit of normal."

My last bit of normal was right when I came home from Robin's and felt the winter air drifting through our kitchen, thinking that a bird had flown in. I was oblivious. That was my last bit of normal. Oblivion.

⟞⟝

Back in my room, I turned on my light and took out a pen and the steno book that Blaire had given me for Christmas. I had no idea where to start, so I began with the lunchroom because it was what flashed in my mind first—food, of course—walking in by myself, my paper bag sweaty in my grasp. Then I thought of the smell of empty milk cartons and icy fudgsicles, which reminded me of summer and sunburns and squeezing lemon on my hair and licking mint chip cones from Gifford's. Words spilled onto the page, my pen leaving stories on the blue lines like magic.

I wrote until the pen dropped from my fingers. I didn't need a jackhammer to break through myself, and I didn't need a psychiatrist to assure me that my morbid thoughts were normal; I'd just needed the truth.

Chapter 26

THE LAKE THAWED. No more thick chunks of floating ice—just small dark waves rushing toward us.

"You think he really wanted to die?" I asked Blaire as we stood on our patch of sand. Her hair was still way too short, but the ends weren't quite as sharp.

"Maybe he just wanted to stop feeling so bad."

"But how could he…" I'd never understand it. *Suicide.* Like a knife slicing into flesh. *My dad committed suicide.* It would take me years to be able to say it.

My ski jacket rustled as I bent down to pick up a speckled stone, which I dropped into my pocket. Next to it was a broken branch that, when held up against the white sky, looked like a stick figure in mid-stride.

I turned to Blaire, who held a clump of dried seaweed in one hand.

"What if it happens to us?" I asked, picturing a dark blanket hovering overhead, one day swooping down and capturing me as I sat, bored, in Math class.

"If I ever get depressed like that, I'll never do what he did," she said.

We locked eyes for longer than a second and I wondered if she was thinking about Mom saying, "There's no guarantee that you'll be okay," meaning *There's a chance that you'll end up like him.*

"Promise?" I said.

"Promise."

I wanted to believe her. I wanted to know for a fact that she'd never sink to that dark place where Dad had been—and that I wouldn't, either—but the fact was, she didn't know for sure. No one knew. Things happened—horrible, unexpected things—and there was nothing you could do about it. All you could hope was that you knew the truth.

I waded into the freezing water, twisting off the top of the glass jar that for almost an entire year I'd kept buried between pairs of balled up socks. I stopped and poured a small pile of light grey ash into my palm, holding out my arm in front of me like I was feeding an animal at the zoo. Slowly my fingers spread apart. The ashes didn't hesitate on the water's surface or fly into the wind; the lake swallowed them in one gulp. I tossed some underhand as if I were throwing a ball to a child all the way in Michigan. They sunk into the water. I did it again and again until every spec was gone.

So now we were together, sort of. It made sense. Finally there was no more wondering about what to do with his ashes. No more debating whether Mom was lying or not. Or if our family would be okay without him.

Our long nightmare was over. And now it was March and, even though the cold air still prickled my skin, spring was coming. I could feel it in my bones.

About the Author

Jamie Holland grew up in Massachusetts, Maryland, Wisconsin, New York, and Texas. Her short stories have appeared in *Antietam Review, Brain Child, Gargoyle, Literary Mama,* and many other journals. She is working on a young adult novel. Since 1986, she and her husband have been living in Washington, DC. They have two teenage girls. Jamie's website is www.jamieholland.org